Rabbit Rebellion

Liam Adams

Cover illustration by Liam Adams

Rabbit Rebellion

by Liam Adams

everyoneneedsaliam.com.au

We think this book is mostly suited to children from 10 years old, and young adults, 12 and over, although older adults may enjoy it as much!

This book is sold on the understanding that it is the work of a person with intellectual disability and Autism. All creativity is from the author and the text has been edited by his mother to the best of her ability. However, it is understood that the writing may be different from that expected in a formally published novel.

Liam hopes you enjoy reading his book as much as he enjoyed writing it. He would love to hear your feedback; if you wish to contact him his email address is ltahm@icloud.com

Canberra, Australia, January 2024

ISBN: 978-0-6455970-4-2

Table of Contents

Preface

The Nature of Rabbits. We may never quite understand them like Human Beings; they are just softballs with long ears and a smaller softball for tails, who normally run very fast. They are a natural and mostly unnoticed species which we really don't focus on.

But what do we normally know of them, really? What do they do while we're not looking? What big secrets lie behind the honest and very reliable eyes they inhabit?

Liam Adams, Rabbit Rebellion

Well, hello again! I wasn't expecting to see you so soon. Let me tell you of the world of rabbits, and what makes them just incredible creatures which us humans find so difficult to understand.

It all came about when I volunteered in a weekly job where I socialised these creatures. I normally sat with one then another, patting and talking to them. It became a weekly thing, until one day I thought, "What if they disagreed with humanity?"

Of course, it was a silly thought; - but what if they did? The Rabbit Rebellion! (Huh, it really just came like that, didn't it?)

Sure, the book just came from a silly concept of rabbits taking a stand against humanity, and I thought, "that can't work." But I noticed, while I spent several months with them, I noticed that a few of them were very different to others.

And I was thinking, "What if they had different perspectives on things? Things that they don't agree on with each other?"

The rabbits in this book are more reliable than humans; they do things that show they are superior, but you still get some who had different opinions.

So, while rabbits are mostly calming and peaceful, you get two of the world's jerkiest rabbit leaders who want to fight for it all! One side shall claim a new ruler, and another gets the same title as before.

A real competition you get for sure! But a rumour gets spread out that a rabbit who isn't so idiotic must end the rabbit rebellion before it ever starts!

While there is loads of silliness happening in the book, I got other ideas in the book, as you'll see. I made the two separate villages with a different feel: one is more farmland, calming and feels like an average town, while another is fully colourful with a big population and so many activities happening.

Then you'll get elements which I planned to combine different types of genres but in rabbit form. It's great to see these rabbits planning out these devious plans on one side or another, which makes this book so readable. I really did enjoy writing the parts where the rabbits on each side were doing these stunts as they really do get out of hand!

I also really enjoyed writing the characters. You'll get some who are really flawed and have bad moods, and others that aren't entirely smart, but they find their own way in the book to earn the reader's affection where you can't help but root for them.

Lots of fun! That's what it is really. It's silly, whimsical fun, where you don't have this sort of wacky in my other books, because…RABBITS!!!!!

I have no idea why I ever thought of writing this. I wasn't thinking it was going to be an actual big thing, but here we are!

I really do hope everyone will enjoy this cracker of a book. Chose which team you would like to win! Who shall claim to be winner? Read on to find out…

Liam Adams, Summer 2024

1. The Rebellion Begins

The Nature of Rabbits. We may never quite understand them like Human Beings; they are just softballs with long ears and smaller softballs for tails, who run very fast. They are a natural and mostly unnoticed species which we really don't focus on.

But what do we know of them, really? What do they do while we're not looking? What big secrets lie behind their honest and very reliable eyes?

Well, beyond what we are told of them, there is an entirely different point of view.

In the 'plain fields' countryside, miles from the city of Brookland, there lay two rabbit villages which were very much a part of each other. These were the main rabbit societies that had been around since medieval times.

Humans and rabbits were not unalike. Rabbits studied humanity and copied human craftsmanship for centuries. For example, rabbits started making bricks and clothes in the same week! Then, the next week, they hired their first very own blacksmith!

Rabbits were way more intelligent and way smarter than humans; that's why they didn't really show it in public, as they knew what humans could become - humans could become quite savage and behave like idiots. That's not just the way rabbits thought of humans; everyone thought of humans that way.

Rabbits had no desire to improve their society, like going to the moon or using Artificial Intelligence to look after their world. Who did that anyway? It would only doom existence!

This was what any rabbit thought of humanity and why they tried to avoid interacting with humans. There were so many reasons why humans were bad, one being that they would keep a rabbit as a prisoner for eternity!

Rabbits went back to ancient times with King Arthur and the Knights of the Round Table. To them this was the Golden Age, where they grew to learn and build and create their own empire. Until humans became boring and stupid. That was a massive difference between these two races, and rabbits now had no desire to live among humans if they had a choice.

Rabbits were not boring or stupid, or making a fool of themselves when they were late to get to work as they were busy late last night as they had a date with their girl friend from the recent football game and lost and had to find a lazy excuses about the whole story and lie.

Rabbits were happy with their social system, and their lives couldn't get any better. And rabbits did a few things that humans would never do. They really focussed on the ecosystem and the whole nature of the world. They produced food, planted trees in farmlands for other rabbits to help different animals in the wild, and sent the message out to help each other and go with the Rabbit System!

"Who?" asked a curious Owl. A rabbit known as Jab of the Rabbit Retrieve was explaining the entire story.

"Ah, well…" the rabbit said as he tried to clear his throat and explain what this Rabbit System was. "It's a system where we tell other animals to look after our planet and gather other animals in your neighbourhood and plant more trees."

"Trees?" the Owl asked again, still a bit unsure about the whole statement this random rabbit was telling him. "Listen, I hardly see anyone, but what are these 'trees' supposed to do?"

The little white and grey furry rabbit gave a promising and cheerful glare towards the owl. He unfolded his statement paper and placed it back in his bag. "The trees carry a supernatural force which protects all of us…."

"You're just theorising that, right?"

"… it's what we all believe; we don't know why we're alive," Jab said as a fact, "but you should tell your friends all about it."

"I don't know anyone," the owl told the rabbit, "I'm a wandering traveller with no destination in sight."

"Oh well," Jab thought dimly, "but you can find some animals around the forests where you are going?"

The owl grew quiet for a second, and then with a startling glare, "You know how difficult it is to find anyone in the middle of nowhere?"

"You can still call out!" the young rabbit said happily.

"But it's the middle of nowhere!"

"You can still call!"

"But there might be wolves, bears all about!"

"You can…you know what, that's a fair point."

"And either way, how are we meant to summon trees?"

"Well…seeds?"

The Owl made eye contact with the rabbit as he asked, "You're new at this?"

"Yes sir! Just reporting for the Rabbit Retrieve!"

The Owl shrugged with narrowing eyes before he took flight. Jab waved at the owl as the young rabbit made his way to the nearest Rabbit Village, which was nearly 2,050 steps away.

Sunset was getting low, and Jab didn't know what might happen to him in the night. After scrawling through a forest and arriving at a wide grassy field, he came to a rabbit village known as Tim Hole Village.

Jab had never been to Tim Hole Village. He came from Carrot Hill Sight Village, where the rabbits planted their crops outside their village. Jab could still remember the smell of the freshness when the carrots were ready for the season. They grew the best of any carrots, he thought.

Tim Hole Village was about as a pleasant town as it could be if you weren't mentioning how crowded and packed it was.

Buildings stacked up like towers with different colours painted on the walls. They had balconies on the second, third and fourth floor levels where different bunnies popped out and you could easily see all the mess they left there. Sometimes they unfolded blankets or even left flags out, which caused the neighbours to nag.

There were signs every thirty feet; it was silly! The signs pointed at all sorts of places and locations in the town. Sometimes they pointed to special events and would only stay there for two days.

Jab was keen to have enough time to explore the village before he started to go back to his hometown. Tim Hole and Carrot Hill Sight were a bit far apart from each other but weren't very far. Like the distance where you were in London and wanted a Cardiff café. It would take Jab and his entire Rabbit Retrieve team about a day and an afternoon lunch to get home.

After exploring, Jab met up with the other Rabbit Retrieve rabbits where they had dropped off their bags at the town's map sign.

What the Rabbit Retrieve did was to go to far lands and tell any animal they saw in their path about how to support and save the world. It was a very important job that rabbits did; it was all about their world and how they lived in it. Now they must give out the message to the rest of the world so they would do the same.

The Retrieve all wore red Leather Jackets with a Badge that had the Retrieve's name on it so nobody could mistake it.

"Jab, it's good you could join us," said Burg. He was in charge of this squad. He made sure that it was his responsibility if anything happened to the rabbits; he would get the blame and have to leave his village if anything happened. Even how hard and unfair this sounded, there were laws that rabbits must follow. The only punishment was to leave their home and never return.

All the Retrieve rabbits were from Carrot Hill Sight, and they joined Jab at the same time. This was their first Retrieve Journey, and judging by how missions went for any Rabbit Retrieve, they did pretty well. Their journey was through the Wildness of Grassy Fields, where they found more rabbits; then into the Snowy Forest, where they almost got attacked by a wolf, but he preferred to give out their message than eat them. And now they were at Tim Hole Village. This would be their last spot until their homecoming after a Thirteen Day Journey.

They were trying to find a good Motel where they could relax, but by how the map was drawn, it wasn't so simple. Rabbits made drawing maps very complicated, as not only did they have exhilarating minds, but they had different pathways and tunnels with arrows pointing all over the place. There were many options; they could go either underground or use one of the surface buildings.

"So, where would be a good place to stop at?" Burg asked the Team. The whole team were all worn out from their adventure, and they just wanted a big good old rest.

"We could use the Rabbit Hole Motel?" said one of the Retrieves.

"Too dusty, I reckon," said another who had a raggy fur. "I tried it once. It didn't quite clean my fur out. And it never has since." That was quite a tragedy, they all thought.

"I'll take your advice there," Burg commented; he wouldn't risk it. "We need somewhere quite easy and simple, where you all can get your minds cleared."

"We could try Grass Hops Hotel on the Eastern Side," Jab suggested, as he pointed to it on the map, which was easy to find. "It's just a few feet away, guys."

The Retrieve looked at each other and thought that wasn't a bad idea, then moved forward to the place Jab mentioned. While they all walked by, Burg turned towards Jab with a surprised but pleased look.

"Good work, Jab," he called with a slight grin. "I think we'll turn you out to be a great Rabbit Retriever!"

"Yes sir," Jab commented back. He didn't salute as the Retrieve weren't really soldiers.

That's what Jab's entire act was: Jab was the helper. He helped out anyone who needed it. If it was a young bunny who needed his toy to be fixed, or to lure a wild wolf away from an animal in peril. He didn't sign up to be part of this team not to help save the planet. He believed in it, and he wanted to make a difference.

The sky was dimming in the village as nightfall dropped. It was a pleasant night, but every night here got noisy. But this was no ordinary night.

Underneath one of Tim Hole's Bars, there were a few rabbits around as they heard the Mayor from Carrot Hill Sight Village was going to have a meeting with their Mayor.

Rag: Mayor of Tim Hole Village, was a rusty and unpleasant rabbit who didn't like waiting or getting the wrong food he ordered. He had distinct ideas as to what he thought was good for his village.

Gabs: Mayor of Carrot Hill Sight, was more secretive to his people than they realized. He sometimes let his second Servant drop out some tiny rumours, to let the rabbits know how much of a great leader he was, even though they were lies.

Besides what they had done for their villages, neither of them were good rabbit as Mayors; they had their struggles, and they knew it well.

Even being distant they didn't have a good relationship and didn't have good agreements; a massive urgent Meeting had to happen. They feared this would happen soon enough, and they didn't want to go with it, but they had very little choice.

Rag was waiting for Gabs to travel to his Village. Rag brought his brother, who was beyond helpless, to massive talks like this. Yossi was cloud-headed even though he tried to be helpful for his brother. It was hard to believe these two were brothers. There was one point during his younger brother's lifetime when Rag got bitten by a snake and his brother spit out the poison like nothing had happened to him.

Yossi was patting his foot very fast, and it was driving his brother nuts. Rag stomped his big fury foot on his brother's foot on purpose.

"Ow," Yossi called out as he felt the pain but didn't have a roaring reaction.

Rag grumbled as he looked around the bar, trying to see when Gabs may pop in.

"We don't need this," Rag spoke, who feared the worst. He always had a negative emotion, but he preferred to not mention it.

"Don't say that," Yossi commented brightly, who had a very positive attitude. "We had the fry corn cake when we got here…."

"That's not what I'm saying, Yossi," Rag interrupted, who by this moment was growing nervous by troubling news. "I don't want to be here, but with the crisis we're hearing about, what else can we do?"

Yossi simply glared with no thought.

"Just go easy on it. And try to go with whatever direction it goes. It will be good for our village."

"His village or mine?" As much as Rag had some rough times with his brother, he did care for him. But some days like today he just couldn't stand with Yossi's silliness.

Shortly after, Gabs arrived in the hole with two of his bodyguards in case some rabbits tried to kill him on the spot. He sat on the other side of Rag and Yossi across the table.

The rest of the rabbits in the bar grew quiet but were trying to pretend to be more occupied and not pay attention. They all knew what was happening, but they tried not to think about it.

Two months ago, The Rabbits Ruler Gum O' Rabbit went missing without any trace. No rabbit would either kidnap or kill their beloved Ruler, as no Rabbit would do such a thing. He usually travelled between

Carrot Hill Sight and Tim Hole in a week. But there had been no word or sighting of their Ruler for two months.

And this caused a problem within the rabbit society, because who would become the next Ruler was between the two Mayors, who had very different points of view. And there must be an agreement to discuss who would take on the title of Ruler.

"So, no word of our missing Ruler?" Rag asked Gabs, to which Gabs shook his head doubtfully.

"There has not been any news about him," Gabs said with a sorrowful look. "No rabbit could tell where he went. A few may guess that he must have been killed by the wild."

When Gabs mentioned the word "wild", it made Yossi's fur shiver which it didn't normally do. He hated hearing stories about the wild; he got nightmares about it.

Rag and Yossi felt an appreciation for their Ruler; every rabbit had, and it was not the same now, and it may never be the same again.

"But now we must talk about what we do from here," Gabs said in a serious tone. Rag watched Gabs closely. He knew Gabs always had a trick up his sleeve. "We need to choose to make one of us Ruler, and the other…."

"Be what? A Governor? A Handyman?" Rag interrupted rashly. Gabs never liked those terms; Gabs was a reliable Rabbit, even though there were things he preferred not to hear what other rabbits said about him.

"Well, it puts you back as Mayor," Yossi told his brother, which Rag didn't want to hear from Yossi.

"Rag", Gabs spoke, "this is more than you and I. I know you're very disconnected with this, but this is a very important role. One of us must take that title."

"Yeah, and that will be one of us!"

There was a distance between Rag and Gabs on the table; they didn't need to like one another or what their villages looked like; they just had to work together.

They narrowed their eyes as Gabs spoke up, "You're only making it harder on yourself, Rag."

"But what I see is two possible ways," Rag explained. "One: I get to be Ruler, and you can keep your village, or Two: you become Ruler, and I won't hear the last of it."

Gabs snarled as his ears folded, and his teeth widened. "You don't know what mistake you are making!"

"Oh, I do!" Rag said brashly, as things were getting personal. Neither of them wanted to be second best. They knew this entire talk would only trigger conflict between the two. One wanted more power than the other, and neither of them would surrender it or share it. There was only one way.

Rag and Gabs stared at each other; the poor and horrified Yossi didn't know what to do. They stared for some time as Rag thought clearly, "There's no way around this, is there?"

Gabs didn't move a nudge, he just looked at Rag with nothing nice to say. "No."

Then, a question lured Rag. He needed to pull on the table to get Gabs' full response. "If I become Ruler, what would you do?"

Gabs' eyes moved away for a second until they raised back to Rag; he had nothing to lose. This was going to be the battle that neither of them would want to lose. Besides the recklessness with which Rag would go for that power, Gabs needed that power more than him. "To war."

"And that's what you get!" Rag responded, as the two mayors shook hands.

Gabs got up from his seat as he and his bodyguards exited the bar. The whole room was silent as the rabbits who witnessed it couldn't pretend to do their own thing anymore. Even Yossi couldn't close his mouth.

"You know what you did?!"

"I do," Rag replied, "and I don't regret it."

2.   The News

Jab and the Retrieve spent their last day at Tim Hole Village chilling and exploring the place, and then the next day, they embarked on their journey home. It took them two days to reach Carrot Hill Sight Village and the afternoon sun was setting behind the hills as they arrived.

They could see the hills leading upwards as the farmers were getting their crops out of the holes. Layers and layers of food were lying outside the town. Old fashioned brick-built houses were stacked inside the gates of the village.

Locals came running as they spotted the Retrieve, as everyone knew that they were doing an excellent thing for their community. The rabbits were thrilled as their excitement couldn't be restrained. A thirteen-day mission that could have caused any casualties and they were all able to survive it all.

All the rabbits that came running - about seventy percent of the village population - were either family, friends, teachers, candle makers or those who just wanted to be part of something quite exciting,

They celebrated until nightfall, where the real fun began! Everyone partied like no human could, in hundreds and hundreds of yards. Fireworks burst into the air even though they were only small; lamps were lit in all colours as rabbits danced and hopped onto walls.

All the Retrieves caught up with their friends and family once again after such a massive journey; Jab caught up with his gang: Wallaba, Apples, Penny, and Ricky. They all wanted to know everything about Jab's travels and what he and his Retrieve had encountered.

"Is it true?" Ricky asked Jab with a pretty astounded look. "You really met an actual deer?!"

They heard stories about other creatures from the wild, as rabbits who lived in the villages didn't leave and see the world outside. Deers to them were only legends they heard about in bedtime stories. But hearing it from their best friend seemed so realistic.

"Yeah, I was only a few feet away from it," Jab explained, though it was relatively cool at the time. "We saw it in the woods where we had to stay put as Burg had to handle the situation. It would have probably hit its antlers into me and chased me across all the way across the forest."

Jab's friends all gasped like children, witnessing a new story unfolding before them. "Did it try to eat you?" Penny asked, worried.

"No, no," Jab explained, "it was off in its own territory. We just met in the most unlikely of places."

"That's a relief," Wallaba said, as he took a breath. "I thought that whole story was going to take a very scary turn."

Jab made a small chuckle after he told everything that had happened to him. "That's enough about me, how are you guys? What have I missed?"

It was quite an intriguing question to Jab, even though it had only been two weeks; but to any rabbit, that was like months ago.

"I've started to learn to play the banjo!" Wallaba told Jab.

"Really?" Jab said, who was quite surprised to hear Wallaba pick up such a hobby.

"Yeah, found it lying about."

"I help him out," Apples added, "seeing if I can teach him. Which I cannot."

Apples and Wallaba were quite a strange collection of friends to Jab; they appeared to be the ones who would do something un-rabbit-like and try to do something quite new in their lives.

Penny, on the other hand, kept a watchful eye on them, seeing that no one could get into trouble, and keeping a quite peacefully neutral attitude.

And Ricky felt like a brother to Jab, as he knew him for the longest - since they were bunnies. Ricky was the one who gave Jab helpful advice whenever Jab need it.

"Cropping season is here," Penny told Jab. She was so over excited she couldn't resist: "and all the rabbits are ready to send them to the families and to the wild, and there's this war..."

"War?! What War?!" Jab asked, jumping out of his skin as he heard the word.

"Oh, we should've told him about that first, right?" Wallaba asked the pals with a guilty look.

"Yeah, you're probably right," Apples agreed with Wallaba. "You should've left the banjo bit till later, man."

"Well, we got the news this morning," Penny explained more about the news to Jab. "Carrot Hill Sight is going to war with Tim's Hole."

"But they're the two biggest Rabbit kingdoms in the world!" Jab exclaimed, as he couldn't believe it. "If they fight, where will all the rabbits go if all that we have built is destroyed?!"

"We can go to the wild," Ricky thought.

"But we'll die in the wild!" Jab told them.

"And how do you know?" Apples questioned him.

"Because I've been to the wild!"

"Oh, that's right," Apples thought. "And it's all got to do with Gum O' Rabbit."

Apples couldn't think what war could bring other than annihilation. He never quite understood what anger or rage was; he was pretty much a chill rabbit who didn't care what happened in their world.

As much this news was troubling, this was way more troubling to Jab as his heart couldn't stop bouncing about. Rabbits are a calm and social species; they don't rage out in war and fight one another.

Even though this whole thing was a political issue that made little sense, none of the rabbits could shake the issue that this was happening,

"You're alright, Jab?" Ricky asked him as he sensed the stress on his friend's face.

"No! Why would I be alright?! War is breaking out and I'm hearing this now?!"

"Well, we couldn't wait for too long," Apples replied, "it will start in only five days."

"Five Days?!?!"

Jab thought tonight would be a great celebration, but it wasn't. They were about to go to war in less than a week and nothing was going to change that.

Penny stroked the poor rabbit as he dropped on the ground, while Wallaba played a single tune on his banjo.

3. The Missing Rabbit

Plans had been set in motion. Well, slowly at least. Very soon, the Rabbit Rebellion would begin and the rabbits on both sides would compete in this upcoming battle, whether they liked their leader or not.

Deals and gatherings had also been made because the two leaders weren't going to play nice. As the rabbits may have guessed, this was big time!

Outwards from the two villages, a group of rabbits were heading into the big city. They had got word from spies that they could research some information about Gab's plans for the war. Everyone may have thought this was totally cheating but from the two leader's perspectives: who cared!

The rabbits who entered the city were from Tim Hole Village as Rag's spies. They entered a small hole where a smaller bar was set up. Other rabbits and even cats were chilling in the bar without causing any scene.

The rabbits spotted the rabbit who had the information, who sat not very far from the entrance. The spies walked up to him as it seemed this bunny was waiting for them. He didn't talk much.

"What you got?" asked the leader of the pack, Gary. Again, the bunny didn't say much. "We know you got the package. Can you tell us what it is?"

The bunny looked up. He wasn't looking at the spies but at his two other backups who were behind them. Gary's gang looked at them from behind and noticed these were some big rabbits. They sat down with the messenger and settled.

"Okay," Gary told the messenger, nodding; he knew this game very well. He looked back at his two guys as they left the bar.

The messenger looked at his pal on the right as he left. One of Gary's pals came back inside but it was a different rabbit. The messenger brought two more guys who were skinny.

Gary gave the other big bunny a terminating stare which frightened him enough to leave. They looked back and forth as rabbits came and went, which drove about five more at least on both sides.

"I think we have too many," Gary told the messenger, who agreed Gray was right.

A few more rabbits left the bar. Only two bunnies from Gary's group and two bunnies from the messenger's group were in the bar, while the rest had left and gone home.

"We got everything you need," the messenger finally spoke.

"Yeah and?"

The Messenger look around the room as he narrowed his eyes. "There's this thing with their leader. They know what move he is going to make, but they don't know when. Because he is so secretive."

"What plans do you know that he is making?" Gary asked as the rabbits from both sides were giving a little suss on each other, trying to figure out what other information they were hiding.

"What I do know they're planning is: he is planning to lure the armies into the city as their battlefield."

"In the city?!" Gary called in surprise. "This city?!"

The Messenger nodded. "With humans about?!" They all thought sending rabbits onto a human city was bad enough as it was; they couldn't risk them facing a war where they were more likely to get captured by animal control.

As much as Gary wanted to ask why they thought this was a good idea, he had a job to do. "But can you at least tell us where your leader will be in the battle?'

The messenger and his two other pals gave Gary and friends a wondering look as he asked, "You aren't on our side, are you?"

"Depends which side you are on?" Gary asked, giving the same response back. Gary was trying to figure out these rabbits until he realized they were not from Tim Hole Village.

The messenger threw carrot knives at Gary and his gang. He flipped the table over as he and his pals raced out on the street while making a retreat.

"FOR GABS!!!! WHO SHALL BE OUR GREATEST RULER FOREVER!!!!!" the messenger called out as they ran very fast.

Gary and his pals got up. He noticed that one of the knives was stuck on his shoulder for a moment until it dropped off. He also noticed that the knife wasn't dangerous, it was only a distraction to draw their attention while the other rabbits made their escape.

Two days passed while Jab couldn't go back to his daily routine. He just couldn't accept that their world was changing in the most wrong way possible. Besides being a Retrieve, Jab's job was being a farmer. He had to check the crops he planted and take out carrots; it was a simple life.

Now that wasn't the case. He saw rabbits getting ready for the upcoming battle and volunteered to join. They practiced riding on chickens and whacking jousting carrots swords at each other and trying on red leather armour.

Since when did Rabbits choose to fight to the death? There hadn't been a rabbit battle for thousands of years, which was from a disagreement where one of them forgot to not flood the entire crop with too much extra water. They still wondered whose fault it was to this day.

When Jab got back home, he checked the chickens in the pen. They weren't the smartest of animals. They gave a weird reaction to everyone; they just didn't know what the rabbits were to them.

Jab didn't want this war to happen, but the only thing he could do besides doing chores around the village was to socialise with the chickens. It wasn't a solution to their crisis but what else would be? They looked at him with one eye as they couldn't tell why he came to them, but they knew he wasn't a local.

"You wouldn't want a war that could destroy all of rabbit kind, would you?" Jab ask them. He knew talking to a chicken was just like talking to yourself, but worse. "Nah, what am I talking about?"

While Jab was moping about, there was mumbling from a wild rabbit. Jab walked out from his pen to check who it was. A dirty fur rabbit with a torn-out coat and a beanie came up from the village mumbling about stuff. He was saying stuff that was completely random like he saw goats float and fishes who ate mankind.

"Uh excuse me?" Jab asked the rabbit.

The rabbit's eyes raised up like he thought he saw the beautiful angel that was about to take him away, but it wasn't.

"Ah yes!" he commented, "How can I help ya?"

"What are you doing here?" Jab asked him.

The rabbit looked lost and tried to concentrate for a moment. "Just off on the road."

He was a rogue rabbit, Jab thought. They are all sorts of rabbits on the road across the world.

"Sorry to disturb you," Jab said sighing, "it's just been a rough couple of days for us. I think you might've heard the news then. Our ruler is missing, probably dead."

"Dead?" the rabbit asked with a narrow eye gazing on the young bunny. "You think he is dead?"

"He is, isn't he?'

"Well, I can see what's making all you lot so mopey, but what if told you I know where he is?"

Jab pulled his ears back as he paid complete attention.

"Ah yes!" the rabbit told him, as he focussed on Jab's interest. "He is far more alive. Well, at least at the moment."

"How do you know that?" Jab questioned him.

"Have you ever been to the human city?"

"What?! No!" Jab commented, frightened.

"Thought so," the rabbit said, not surprised, "rabbits like you try to avoid that sort of thing."

"It's a policy," Jab thought. He knew it was entirely restricted, and more to the point, illegal. Rogue rabbits were known more as outlaws, the ones who were forced to leave.

"All right," the rabbit said. Jab could tell that he did know what he was talking about. He was willing to hear it all. "He didn't really expect what was going to happen to himself."

"What you mean?"

The rabbit froze as he forgot about a very important detail in the story. "Ah well," he said as he tried to catch his words, "he…he has an owner."

"WHAAAAAT?!" Jab cried. Jab knew that their ruler would never go to the human city unless it wasn't by his own wishes. But also, an owner?!

Then a question struck him which terrified the young rabbit, "Was he…happy?"

"Oh, delightfully," the rabbit commented, as it gave Jab shivers. There were stories about if you ever encountered humans. They took you with them and you become their prisoner forever and you got used to it and started to like it. "He has been treated nicely, being calm, relaxed, and having every luxury he can ever have...."

"Stop, Stop!" Jab told the rabbit as he couldn't bear to hear it. His heart was bouncing as fast as it had ever gone before. "Where did you find him?!"

"On Second Three Dion Avenue. Quite an ordinary street. I imagine whoever got him has him good."

"Please, Stop!!" Jab told him as he thought he couldn't take anymore. "I'll have to tell somebody!" he said as he raced out.

As much as it was hard for the truth to be told, Gum O' Rabbit was indeed enjoying himself. He quite liked the company of humans if you got to know them better. He stayed in an apartment on one of the highest floors where he could gaze upon the human city. His owner - forty-three-year-old Quantise Clan - who wasn't much more than a fool who had many hobbies: music, karate, cooking, and other random things that the rabbit couldn't keep up with.

Quantise was busy singing to himself as he was practicing few vocal sounds which sounded like they needed some work; Gum was taking a nap through all of this as he thought his owner had quite a symphony in his voice.

It should have been sadder for any pet to be accompanied by a guy who could not only not play the piano but did bad karate. But Gum was quite happy about it all. He was a very old rabbit if you must know. A few rabbits said that he had been alive for nearly forty years which was not true.

As much as Gum knew that Quantise was pushing himself a little too hard, he supported Quantise in whatever he wanted. But what Gum should be thinking about was his colony and how they would react to his disappearance. There were greater things to think about than taking a nap and having nothing to do, but that thought never crossed his mind.

4.   Rabbit Trouble

Jab tried to reach to any of his pals in the nearby neighbourhood; the only bad news was that not a lot of them were around. He noticed a few rabbits were volunteering to fight, which drove him into a hassle.

He knocked at his friends' doors in an extreme haste. As rabbits, they sped along about five times faster than a human, but if a human was that fast, they could die. You may also be thinking that rabbits could get tired from that sort of energy, but they don't.

Jab was rushing all over the places he could think of until he could spot one of them. Somewhere quite quiet, he saw Ricky all by himself.

"Ricky!!!!!!" he cried out.

Ricky turned around and looked at Jab, in relief but also quite confused.

"Jab!" Ricky called back. "What's up?"

When Jab reached Ricky, he was dripping with sweat, and he had full expression of urgency that gave Ricky some odd thoughts.

"You haven't been drinking from the barrow near the chicken pen, have you?" Ricky asked him. "You know you're not supposed to drink that."

"This isn't about the stupid chicken pen! Anyway, gross!" Jab replied back, disgusted. "This is about Gum O' Rabbit!"

"The Ruler?" Ricky asked confused. "Isn't he meant to be lost?"

"He isn't lost. Well, what I heard he isn't lost," Jab explained. "I've talked to a rogue rabbit, you see. He said…."

"Jab, you shouldn't go around and talk to rogue rabbits that aren't from the city," Ricky told him.

"But he said he saw him!" Jab said, who felt that the story may slowly be becoming true. "He said that he encountered him in the human city, where he's being held captive."

"Jab," Ricky stopped him, "you know we can't go out into the human city, right? You're a member of the Rabbit Retrieve; you know that it's a policy to stay as far away from any human environment as possible."

"But he can stop this war!" Jab told Ricky to get his priorities right. He knew his pals were likely to avoid being involved in anything so major, but Jab couldn't help it, he knew nothing was going to change unless he took that chance.

A cough came behind them and they noticed it was the Retrieve leader, Burg who gave them a very terminating look.

Jab gave him a shy look, "Uh, hi."

Burg took the two to the most unexpected place - that being the Mayor's building, which was a stack in the town with two floors. Gab's office was on the second floor where Burg opened the door for Jab and Ricky. It was a wide enough room with a plain office desk with shelves. There was also a large round window behind the desk where they could see a view of the entire town. The only rabbit inside the room beside the three was Gabs, who had recently heard of this unexpected news.

"Alive?" Gabs asked Jab after hearing that there was a slight possibility that their missing leader was still alive. "You have any evidence for this?'

There wasn't much to go on other than the rumour. Jab couldn't add anything further than what Burg had reported. "Well, no."

"Then why were you two talking about this as if it was so major?" the Mayor asked, who thought the story was becoming so large his ears were ringing.

Ricky lifted his arm up. "Well, I haven't got anything to do with anything, sir."

"No, no," Gabs said, as he waved his hand at Ricky to put his arm down. "We'll let you go after we know what you were on about."

Jab didn't share the full story about Gum O' Rabbit being alive, and he sure didn't tell them where he was. "We also have heard that Gum might be in the human city."

"Then why would he be there?" Gabs asked. It wouldn't make sense why any rabbit like their ruler would be going around to a forbidden place as that.

"He might be taken." Jab told Gabs.

"Taken?" Burg butted in. "Like humans took him?"

Gabs raised his eyebrows with an astonishing look. "This is some serious information," Gabs said to the young rabbit. "No human could reach our villages. We know how far apart we are from them. Besides, how could one human come here?"

It was distant, but Jab knew anything was quite possible. If he and the rest of the Retrieve made their way going to distant lands and encountered other animals, why would it be any different for humans to manage to kidnap their leader on a regular walk?

"But it could be possible!" Jab tried to reason. "Send out a search party! Search every ground!"

"Towards the human city?!" Gabs said, so astonished he cannot believe what he was hearing from a rabbit from his village. It sounded like he was talking to a rogue rabbit.

"Jab," Burg said, in a rough but soft tone, "you should reconsider what you're thinking."

"But you can't ignore this!" Jab said. He thought what they were doing was wrong, not what he was proposing. "Gum can end this!"

"So, it all leads to our war, doesn't it?" Gabs thought it sounded like nothing but a rabbit trying to stop the war. "It isn't as simple as that."

"Because you're not trying hard enough!" Then it struck him. Jab was going more overboard than he realised and he knew he was out of his limits.

He restrained himself as he went quiet and made an apologetic look, "I'm sorry, Lord Gabs."

"Then that settles it then," Gabs said as he gazed out the window, "it's nothing more than a simple rabbit posing a fake theory, trying to put an end to this war."

"But…" Jab tried to cut in before Burg gave Jab a serious look to step outside. Jab followed that instruction as he and Ricky left the room.

But before they did so, Gabs had one last thing to add. "But to let you know, this isn't personal."

Meanwhile, back at Tim Hole Village, there was a jousting carnival, where rabbits were watching a new prototype of the chicken riders. It wasn't just for fun; this gave the rabbits a closer look at how these inventions would be useful in a battle.

The riders wore purple leather armour and a helmet. They also had a jousting sword and rode their chickens. They were on far opposite ends where they soon met in the middle in a mighty clash. The rabbits weren't totally brave because they knew one or the other might get wrecked in the session.

Gary was part of the crowd as well as Rag and Yossi. Yossi was eating popcorn as he watched the crowd for the torment, while Rag and Gary were in deep conversation.

"What is this Gabs doing?" Rag asked Gary about the other night.

"I'm not sure." Gary shrugged as he didn't know what the other Mayor was like. "If you won't mind me saying: I think he is trying to outsmart you."

What Rag didn't like more than anything else was being tricked. Gabs was the smart one and Rag was the one with issues. He knew how to strike him without trying. He knew if you had someone who didn't behave, he knew how to punish.

This angered Rag as he knew this was Gabs' first act of attack against him personally. "We can't let Gabs win," he said, knowing that losing would be a terrible embarrassment for himself. "I won't let that rabbit get his paws on a chance to become Ruler!"

"Well, you could let him…" Yossi thought nicely, while Rag threw his popcorn away.

"You want to add anything else?" Rag asked his brother. Yossi's head shook. Rag looked back at Gary as the Jousting round began. "Anyway, I think I know just the right plan that Gabs doesn't know about that I will be playing in the battlefield."

"Do you?" Gary and Yossi asked.

"Yes." Rag corrected them. "Don't let Gabs be the only one who has clever strategies during this war. I have few of my own to play on him."

Then Yossi thought to himself for a moment; he knew what plans Rag had lined up. "Oh yeah!"

Gary sat quietly as he was about to take his leave. "If you don't mind, Rag. I think our meeting has adjourned."

"All right, off you go!" Rag dismissed the spy while one of the jousters fell off his chicken by the carrot sword of his opponent. He got up and let the crowd know that he was alright.

5. Rag's Secret Weapons

Elsewhere in the snowy mountains across many thousands of miles and scary heights away, another messenger from Tim Hole Village journeyed with a companion. He was scared; he wasn't sure how he would go with the extreme exhaustion caused by travelling up a cold mountain.

They were sent couple days ago from Rag, who knew it would take them a while to reach their destination, but they're objective was to be all ready for battle.

At the Academy of Bunny Marshal Arts and Mastery of Skills, these were rabbits who could move in shadows, trained fighters performing epic stunts and any other thing you could throw at them. They were your best weapons.

As they were not soldiers, they were an isolated group on their own. But Rag needed help from well-trained rabbits who aren't any noobs with big carrots.

The messenger entered inside, and he saw a whole room where the rabbits trained to their fullest. The messenger saw them dodging attacks, throwing carrot daggers at carboard targets and amazing stunts that made the messenger's eyes blink and think that he may miss it.

"Yes." spoke the Chief of the Academy, which startled the messenger.

"Yes!" the messenger replied. He pulled out a scroll Rag wrote and passed it over to the Chief. "Rag from Tim Hole Village wanted me to give you this."

"Rag?" the Chief asked as he raised an eyebrow, "Is he the small one with grey fur?"

"No sir."

"Hmm," the Chief said as he read the scroll. It told him Rag needed his Samurais in this upcoming battle as they would be very useful. Rag left out saying that he had the worst fear that Gabs would easily defeat him, and they may lose anyway.

"Very well, I shall lend you my students."

"Thanks." the messenger replied. "Uh, how many?"

"All of them." the Chief said, as all the students stopped their training and gathered in the room in the centre. They stood still as they waited for instructions.

The messenger looked quite overwhelmed to see how focussed they were. "You, uh, have quite the students."

"The very best." the Chief told him. "If Rag needs an army, he'll get one."

"Thank you." the messenger said nervously, "I'll report to Rag right away about this!"

"Yes, you do that." The Chief didn't give the rabbit the hospitality to stay to have a drink after his journey or stay for the night. The Chief was too busy with the students training to observe any outsider. The messenger left as he and his friend took their leave.

Night fell on the day, while in the human city, Quantise was asleep as Gum sat quietly. Gum knew the habits Quantise brought to his life. As much he supported his actions and desires, he was mainly a dork.

Gum knew a way to sneak out of his cage which wasn't so hard for any rabbit to solve. He leant over to the handles on the other side of the cage, and it suddenly slid open.

Gum went and walked over to the window where he tried to gaze upon the city, hoping to see the grassy fields. He did this for a few nights as he thought of his rabbits. He knew deep down that he had a big responsibility that he could not throw away; rather, he liked it. He thought everything was going fine over there, but there was a tingling sense that he couldn't shake, like something bad was happening.

He did not know what the rabbits may do while he wasn't with them. He did know there would be a big conflict in which the rabbits would have to make difficult decisions. This troubled Gum for sure, but he knew he couldn't leave his quirky and disappointing Quantise. He saw so much greatness in him which surprised the Ruler.

Gum looked back to his owner, all in his deep sleep. Gum walked over to him and put a paw on his hair. There was a strange connection between the rabbit and his owner, but Gum never quite understood it till tonight. He later put his paw away and started chewing on his owner's hair. His owner was still asleep; now he was dreaming he was in the best candy store he had ever stepped into, while the Candyman was giving him some treats.

"Hmm, candy," Quantise said dreamily.

Gum never understood some words that humans said. He knew stuff like "building" or "government." But not anything like "candy" or "train stations." This world was just too much for a rabbit.

During the late night, Jab and Ricky joined their pals in the Jolly Pen underneath the town, where rabbits came to chill out. A lot of the time, it was a party house where every rabbit could go wild, which caused a mess.

They told them everything that happened in the last few hours. They were both stunned but also quite down.

"I can't believe this," Penny said outlandishly, "how could they ignore something so big as this?"

"That's what Jab has been trying to say." Ricky explained. "It looks like they don't want to find our Ruler."

"Who wouldn't?" Wallaba asked, to which all Jab's pals gave a 'not surprised' look as they knew their Mayors were fools.

Jab wasn't in the mood to be drinking with his pals. He was so bothered with everything because he could see the solution, but they let it hop away.

"I just can't go with this!" Jab snapped out of rage.

"We can't do anything about it." Ricky told him trying to support him. "You know this is how it works now."

"This?" Jab said, chuckling like he heard a bad joke. "You really think this war will change anything?" His friends said nothing and grew in silence.

Jab sighed as he never been so hard on anyone, even his friends. "I'm sorry." he apologised deeply. "All I ever want to do is to help. To help rabbits, our rabbits. Now look at it."

Even though it was hard for them, the pals do agree with their friend. Everything has changed for the worse. They don't want it, but how can they reject any of it?

"Jab," Ricky said to Jab. Jab looked at him straight in the eyes, "I haven't given up on you."

"Me too." Wallaba butted in.

"All of us." Penny added.

"You're right." Ricky continued. "I know I tried to push you down earlier, but we can't leave our people in a state like this. But we're not like you."

"You don't have to be like me." Jab told them. "But you can help me. Help me to save all of us."

The five of them stared at each other as they decided they were willing to go on an adventure of a lifetime, which was way too big for them.

"If you think Gum O' Rabbit is out there, I don't know how you could manage it on your own," Ricky commented. "I'll go with you all the way!"

"Thank you." Jab replied. "You think you all can manage?"

"No," Apples blushed, to which Penny butted him in the head. "Uh, yeah. I think?"

"Then let's save the rabbit race!"

6. Out of Town

Jab and the other rabbits ran past their village and raced through the grass which brushed into their faces. They ran to think about where the human city was. They shortly came to a stop as they came to a road that wasn't something they were all familiar with.

"Is this where the pathway to the human city goes?" Apples asked Jab who he knew had more knowledge than himself.

Jab looked both ways. His best guess was as good as any other guess.

"I think so," he replied. He and the others regrouped away from the path. "Remember, we have only a single day till the war begins. It won't be easy, it won't be safe, but this is our only chance to save our kind."

"You're speaking so intensely!" Apples commented, who thought Jab was getting over-dramatic.

"But he is right." Ricky told Apples. "We have limited time remaining. We have to be swift!"

"And there's this," Jab looked back at the road, "I'm not sure what they have around here. But some bunnies did say there's this thing that moves very fast."

"What thing?!" Apples asked terrified.

"Is it dangerous?" Wallaba asked.

"Everything in the human city is dangerous." Jab told them. "Whenever we see it, whatever it is, jump!"

"JUMP?!" they all called.

"Yes, jump!"

No-one was entirely so sure of themselves; they thought this was a bad idea. But if it was, they needed to get into the city, and there wasn't a better way getting there than this.

Just then, a bright light came from the right at extreme speed. They realised that this would be their ride.

"Alright, jum…" tried Jab. But before he could say the word, the car passed them, and they missed it.

They watched it go by as they stood still in silence with the cracking cricket noises around them.

"When does the next one come?" Apples asked.

Then another light was coming, and they thought this wasn't a moment they could miss.

"NOW!!!" Jab called as they all jumped.

When they got onto the car's back, it was all shinny and slippery and they tried to get their big feet running on top of the roof. Wallaba was having difficulty as he didn't have as much energy as the other rabbits. He was sliding down and was about to fall. Penny caught Wallaba by the foot and wielded him up with the others.

"Uh, thanks for that, Penny." Wallaba told Penny, who was shy.

"Don't beat yourself up, Wallaba." Penny told him very brightly. "Not every rabbit can get used to these environments."

"Well, I sure don't." Wallaba said. He thought the world was stranger than he knew.

"Well, welcome to the club, buddy!" Apples told him.

"Hey, look!" Ricky called. They could see the city on the horizon. They all gasped and were blown away to see how massive it was. It was also unreal and very big. This was their chance to discover and see what it was like in the human city.

"Is that where the humans live?" Penny asked in amazement.

"Looks like it." Jab replied.

"It's beautiful."

"It's deadly!" Apples said. He was the only one who was frightened to death to enter the city. If there was one rabbit of the five who wanted to be left behind in Carrot Hill Sight, it was him.

The car took them directly to the city. They all braced for whatever was about to await them.

It was close to nine when Rag tried to get measured by his brother for a new dressing down, when he heard some news from Carrot Hill Sight.

"A rabbit thinks he heard our missing Ruler has been found?!" Rag asked in a quite surprised tone, while standing very still.

"It was a little rumour that was going around this morning that a few of the spies from Gabs' village have been hearing." Yossi explained. "Shall I tell Gary to kill him for you?" he asked nicely.

"No!" Rag snapped as he rolled his head. It wasn't an emotion of annoyance but concern. "What's with you and these ideas?"

Yossi looked up at his brother and said, "I thought you would want that?"

"No, I don't want that. Anyway, why would I ever want to kill him?"

"So, you could hide the evidence that our Ruler is still alive, and if the word got out everyone would start to look for him, and you wouldn't get your chance of being Ruler."

"That is entirely true." Rag said, as he agreed with Yossi's thought. He thought Yossi's ideas weren't half bad in most parts. "But he still means so little to me. Besides, no rabbit could survive the city if they have some experience of it."

"Yeah, the city is such a big and dangerous place." Yossi added. "You don't know where you'll be going, fearsome creatures wonder in the shadows, humans everywhere...."

"Ow!" Rag exclaimed as Yossi pulled one of his arms.

"Sorry."

Rag shook his head again and went back into his chair. "How goes our troops?"

Yossi had some reports of the army; he heard they were making progress and still training quite well. "They finally recruited two hundred more by this morning. I've checked."

"Ah good," Rag was pleased, as he had so much more to plan. He only just brushed the surface. It was only a matter of time till it began. "Get them already for their biggest trials tomorrow. And tell them to plan the

diversions in the battlefields. We need full reports at
sundown tomorrow."

"Will do." Yossi confirmed. He would do
anything for his brother. Anything, no matter how much
he would try to get the same affection back from his
brother.

"We have only got one more day to go after this,
Yossi." Rag said. "And then everything's going to
change!"

7.   Plans and Plans

While a lot was going on that very night, Rag wasn't the only bunny who was making plans. Gabs went over to one of his villager's rabbit holes which was owned by a rabbit he had known for a long time.

Perm had been in long-time service to Gum O' Rabbit and was a best friend of Gabs. Gabs had heard stories that Rag had supplies that would build enough of his army. And he had been given word that a few of Rag's spies had enough resources to keep Gabs at bay. Gabs hadn't had enough news about what Rag was going for, which meant he needed to act fast!

Gabs and Perm invited two other rabbits into Perm's living room. They sat around a round table that looked like it was chopped off from a tree and somebody forgot to add any detail to it.

The two rabbits had secret information which gave them shivering news.

"Rag has done it," said one of the rabbits called Fame, who had a soft but speedy voice. "He has a bunch of troops and enough weaponry that we couldn't pin down!"

"What are we going to do?" asked Scottish Dulster, who had white fur.

As much as Gabs had a lot on his plate as it was, this didn't surprise him. He knew Rag was going to give his all if it would allow him to claim to be Number One. Gabs had put so much enough energy into his villagers to prepare for the war, but he had to face the facts: it was not enough.

Gabs straightened himself as his eyes rose up to the three rabbits in the room. "We need a diversion," he responded.

"Do you have one, Gabs?" Perm asked.

Gabs did. He had come up with it all in one day, but he had never shared it with any other rabbit, except for the ones he was about to tell in the room right now.

"I do," he said, feeling very reliable that this plan will work no matter what, "but I wanted to hear what you all had in mind?"

The group looked at one another then looked back at Gabs.

Dulster explained his idea, "So, we have this show that everyone would come to, then we go and try to move it away from the village…"

"How do we do that?" Fame asked from next to him.

Dulster paused for just a moment as he came with the answer, "We turn it invisible!"

The rabbits gave a questionable stare at Dulster as they knew not to choose Dulster to come up with a clever plan. "You see? We turn the whole show invisible so no one can find them…"

"I like what you're thinking Dulster but I don't think that would do," Gabs announced poorly, as turning a show invisible wasn't going to get them his vote, so Dulster's idea was out.

Gabs looked at Fame as he wanted to hear what she wanted to bring to the table.

"We could send some stealth soldiers to go in the village and pretend to help out the troops, while they steal their weapons."

"Good work, Fame, good work!" Gabs applauded, as he liked what she had to offer; it was much better. "But it would take up a lot of time to hire the right rabbits, which is time we don't have. – You!"

A Rabbit was in the room as he hopped over to eat some briskets; he was a rusty rabbit with strange, wicked eyes. He nibbled one bit then another while he noticed Gabs was staring at him.

"What do you have to offer?" Gabs demanded.

"Oh, I live here," the rabbit said as he left the room. Gabs shook his head reminding himself not to allow Perm to let his housemate into these sorts of meetings.

Then after hearing what the other rabbits had to say, Gabs laid out his master plan.

Then Perm's brother came back into the room.

"Get out," Gabs told him and the rabbit did so.

The Blue Jersey car entered the larger city of Brookland. The driver had no idea what was above him. The rabbits were stunned as they realised the human world was enormous. They saw giant skyscrapers, billboards, streetlights, and a bunch of cars. It was full of colour and human people walked all over the place. Few noticed the rabbits on the Blue Jersey roof, all of whom were quite confused.

The rabbits had nothing to do but look in amazement. It was much bigger than they could ever imagine, and by the looks of things, it was a truly incredible feeling.

"Wow! It's beautiful!" Penny commented as their eyes couldn't take in what they were witnessing.

"Beautiful, you say?" Apples asked Penny. "I say it's all too shiny in my opinion."

Even though it was hard to compare with Apple's comment, Penny was right. The city was massive, streetlights went on for miles and there were about a dozen roads and so many people.

"Rad," Wallaba commented, while nodding his head up and down. This was such a strange and incredible place; they had no idea what to think anymore. Wallaba decided he wanted to greet the driver and he dropped down to the window.

Jab quickly noticed him what he was going to do and grabbed his friend's leg pulling him back up just in time.

"Nonononono," Jab told him as he brought Wallaba back. "We can't have any contact with humans."

"Why not?" Penny asked. She seemed to think humans were almost like any simple animal they had encountered before. "They seem nice."

"I don't get why they're bad." Wallaba wondered as he didn't get the context.

"Have you guys forgotten why we were strictly forbidden to encounter them?!" Ricky asked them, quite shocked and surprised. He knew they should recall this from when they were brought up.

"It's because Rabbits have rights, and humans don't know that," Jab told them. "They keep you and feed you, but you don't explore the fields or go and have meals with friends."

"like…a pet?" Wallaba mentioned that cursed word.

"Exactly!" This horrified the rabbits. Not because they would have a bad life but because rabbits were built for nature and outdoors. They had a purpose, and they knew humans didn't know it. But rabbits from the Village side who had spent so much time with their own kind would get home-sick.

As much as they didn't know where they were going, Jab was hoping there would be a street that might be good to jump off and check where they could find a map or something, but Apples thought this was too much.

Lights! Too Many Street Lights! Turning Green, Yellow, Red! Red! REEEEEDDD!!!!! "I Can't take it!" Apples called out as he jumped off the car.

All the rabbits watched him hop over the traffic as cars hit their breaks. They watched in horror as they saw their dearest friend survive the wild road.

"What is that fool doing?!" Ricky asked, a bit outraged.

"I have no idea what was driving him," Jabs commented, calmly, "but what I do know is that every animal has their own reaction to things. And we have to chase after him, come on!"

The rabbits leapt to the nearest car roof and continued to jump onto another which drove in Apples' direction.

Apples was busy trying to stay alive. He couldn't jump on board and go to another place so fast. He never understood the human world, he never expected it would be like this, and now he was running for his life with no expectation of what may happen next.

The group of rabbits kept jumping on the cars as they followed Apple's trail. But he seemed to notice that he was making a trail of his own as cars stacked up like a mess.

"Now what?" Wallaba asked, as there wasn't any way to get through.

"What you think?" Jab asked, as he noticed that jumping on so many cars was like jumping on tall rocks. Jab raced towards the roofs and his pals joined him. They jumped on one roof after the other as they found another car which wasn't stuck but was going near them.

"Up ahead!" Jab called so they couldn't miss it. They all jumped on the car as it drove towards Apples.

Apples was racing as fast as cars were stopping. Shortly he came to a pathway where people were walking by and sitting down. He avoided them and hopped over the many obstacles they were carrying. People shrieked as they wondered how a rabbit came to be in such a place. He later returned to the road where Jab and his pals saw him, but it was still hard for them to reach him.

"Apples!" Penny called out. "You have to stop and relax!"

"How can I?!" Apples raised his voice. Sweat was draining him down. "How can I relax in a big city with nobs and fur heads?!"

They realised that they couldn't stop him in a place like this. Jab though of a weird idea which could save his friend's life, but also may harm both himself and Apples. He bounced off the roof and glided over to Apples. They clashed and rolled over.

They continued to roll over until they reached a gap in an alleyway where they fell.

"No!" Ricky cried. The rest of them gasped as they had no idea what happened to their friends. The car drove them away so they would have to find another way to reach their friends.

8.   Oh, Mow!

The night grew quiet for Gum O' Rabbit, where he had the whole house to himself. His owner snored all night and couldn't stay awake for one moment! Gum had no issue with Quantise except when his owner was sleeping.

He thought he could tap his Owner on the nose, and it would stop the snoring. It only stopped for about a second and a half until he made another snore. Gum started to tap more, which seemed more like he was hitting the nose.

Quantise started to sneeze, which blew Gum away. Gum backed away into his cage and closed it.

The leader couldn't take another night if his owner decided to sleep again on the couch rather than on the bed. But again, the leader took pleasure in being with his owner, no matter what issues he had with him.

A Pigeon usually came to their window to annoy the Ruler. Gum had to respect that bird even though the rabbit had higher powers than his. The bird always wanted to be a real jerk because he could spy on other animals in the city, and he had more freedom than the rest.

Gum looked at the bird to give him a warning.

"Back off!" he called slowly and quietly.

The pigeon did so but Gum thought this will not be the last time he would see him.

Apples and Jab were rolling and falling thirty feet until they landed in a garbage heap. As they entered the gutter, there was filthy trash all over the place. It was not clean, and the neighbourhood was deserted.

"Aguugh," Jab moaned as he noticed a banana peel on Apples' head. Jab wanted to help him to take it off his head but only if he wasn't in a bad mood already, "What was all that about?!"

"I'm sorry, Ok?" Apples tried to be apologetic, but he knew he couldn't. "You just made things happen way too quickly for me. I needed to take one step after the other, not race things to the end."

"We've got a mission," Jab reminded him.

"You got a mission; I just wanted to stay home."

"Then why did you tag along?"

There was a sudden pause for the rabbit. "Because I wanted to stay away from the war…okay, I did want to help out."

"Okay," Jab commented, as he tried not to create an augment with his friend. Their friendship was anything but random. They met each other in the strangest parts, on the strangest day and later wanted to join a pinball club and become best buddies.

Jab ignored Apples as he tried to find a way to get out of the gutter. There wasn't an easy way out, as they couldn't tell how far they dropped.

He noticed the walls were taller than they were and seemed like it might be hard to climb. "How you suppose we could get up there?" Apples asked Jab.

"I'm thinking," Jab responded. Then he thought he might test a theory. Jab tried to lean his big foot against the gutter wall, but he fell backwards.

"Oh great," Apples commented, "now, how are we meant to get out of this mess?"

"I'm coming up with it." He got Apples to aid him as Jab had to hop on him and try to reach up. But they never realised how deep they went. Someone added more junk to the trash.

"This isn't getting us anywhere!" Apples told Jab, thinking the odds were too narrow.

"We're not giving up!"

While Jab and Apples tried to try out another plan, they could hear a weird sound passing by near them.

"You hear that?" Jab asked Apples.

It wasn't a normal sound they had encountered before. It was a sound that you could hear if everything was quiet, and you might find it around the closest bar, and it would go away afterwards.

The voices came from skinny and leany animals who were at least a few feet tall and wider than the rabbits. They had black, half orange with whiteness and dark grey fur. They skulked towards the gutter as their scent rose up.

The animals popped their heads above the gutter to stare down at the small fur balls. What Jab and Apples noticed about them was that they had short pointy ears and whiskers. Jab noticed that this was an animal that he hadn't met before.

"Well, well, well," commented the orange-white fur cat teasing them. "Looks like we have a few lost rabbits in the gutter."

"This will be a fine night, friends," the grey cat said, as they prepared to save their meals for dinner.

"Uh, can you help us out?" Jab asked them.

The cats shared confused looks and one asked, "Say what again?"

"Help out?" Jab repeated himself.

Cats knew that if any small creature approached them, they would be in a world of trouble, but they had no idea how a single rabbit wouldn't feel threatened. This one wasn't.

"Look, see we are trying to find some sort of object which can get us out of this mess." explained Jab.

"Doesn't he know about the danger he will get into if he was around us?" the black cat asked the other two cats.

"I don't think they know," the orange-white fur cat said.

The grey cat shrugged his head. He knew if they did plan to eat them, they would like their prey to know the danger than not know. So, the grey cat added "What do you need?"

"Anything!!!!" Jab yelled, while the cats searched for something. Apples was suspicious of the felines by the minute; but he couldn't pinpoint if they were friends or enemies or food.

The cats later returned with a loose wire which allowed the rabbits to climb up. As they met the felines up close "Why were you in there?" asked the silky orange and white cat.

"It's a long story," Jab told them to keep it short.

"Well, I haven't seen a rabbit trapped in a dumpster before," the grey cat said.

But cats don't normally see rabbits at all; seeing them on the streets was very uncommon. "It looks like you guys have come a long way."

"Like I said: it's a long story."

"Anyway, you should keep your ground."

"What do you mean?" Jab asked curiously.

The cat gave a look like he was hiding something from them, but he didn't want to step on the rabbits' feet.

"Well let's say this isn't the most safest of times throughout the day," the cat mentioned. "The street could become quite unexpected at times."

"I can understand that easily!" Apples commented from the back, with the two cats behind him, still figuring out what their deal was.

Then a random thought came to Jab as he took notice of the cat. They were wild; he hadn't seen any animal so wild before. He thought he should ask just to be safe, "You're not half-wolf, are you?"

The cat looked confused, "What's a wolf?"

"You don't want to know," Jab advised them, thinking he should warn about wolves. But he didn't want any other animal knowing about such a terrifying beast in the world. "They would be the least of your trouble here."

"You say," the cat commented like he was trying to be funny. He wondered if a wolf was some kind of cat relative which didn't ring a bell.

They kept walking down the alley and Apples could tell something was off with these cats. It gave him too much of a mystery that he couldn't solve. There was also a distant feeling about them, a feeling that you should not get attached to.

Apples went over to Jab as he was the only rabbit he knew in the neighbourhood. If there was something Apples couldn't cope with or withstand, it was being in the city.

Their friends started to search for them, and they arrived in another alley that went deeper. They were horrified when they saw Jab and Apples fall into darkness. This was the only place that was close to finding them.

The pathway went down a steep ground that almost went towards the sewers. They saw empty boxes and a sewer tunnel behind them. It was also foggy, with a lamp in the distance.

Wallaba bumped into a box, and it collapsed with other packages on top of it. A man in one of the buildings shouted in frustration.

"Sorry!" Wallaba called out to whoever it was.

They called for Jab and Apples, but there were no responses from them.

"Where are they?" Penny asked, as she grew more worried.

Ricky shrugged his head. "No idea," he commented, "but we have to keep going. They might be dying for all we know."

"Maybe don't bring that image into my head," Penny sighed.

"Sorry."

They dug deeper and they felt they were drawing closer to a more dangerous territory. They went past a lamp and noticed the street was so dark they couldn't see anything. It was like entering into pitch black which felt unreal and not so friendly.

"Dude, where's my foot?" Wallaba asked as he couldn't see a thing.

"It's still there; it's just dark, that's all."

"Oh."

"Hmm?"

There was something strange about that last line. It wasn't any of their voices. It was a stealthy voice that was calm and suspicious. The group noticed that. It was easy to also notice they were not alone.

9. Into the Cat House

Wallaba, Ricky and Penny were taken by eighteen Rogue Cats who weren't as pretty as the other three that Jab and Apples were with. Ricky and the others arrived at a street wall near the Old Abandoned Mansion that the Cats had taken over; the Cat House, they call it.

These cats took no notes from the human world. They ran things and made the rules around these streets. This was their big town, and no one was going to take it, not even little rabbits.

The rabbits themselves felt cornered, having so slim a chance of escaping. They never imagined a scenario like this would ever happen in the city. They didn't have any knowledge about what it was really like to be here.

Ricky turned to his friends with a scared look. "I might see you guys at the end of this?" he asked, very frightened. His friends said nothing but hummed. They closed their eyes as the cats growled and were ready to pounce on them.

Until, that is, a firmer voice spoke which gave them beyond any hope: "Hey guys!" No, it couldn't be, but they all opened their eyes and saw Jab and Apples making their way towards them.

The rogue cats backed away from the three rabbits as Jab and Apples made their way towards them, without realizing the full terror that their friends had been through.

But Apples had a strange gut feeling that something was going on.

The grey cat gave the other cats a look that told them, 'Better not feed off them tonight fellas, but maybe another night.'

All the cats listened to that demand, although that seemed wasteful to their mind.

The three rabbits were still in horror and shocked about how they're friends could still be alive with these creatures.

"Jab? Apples?" Ricky said stunned.

"It's good to see you too, old friend," Jab replied, and added a smile, which Ricky and the others shared as well. Apples gave a look of terror at all the cats, thinking they may eat them all. "Hey, they said we could stay here for the night."

"STAY?!" all three rabbits said in as much shock as Apples. They thought they would all be dead if they keep lurking around the area, just like they thought they were goners not so long ago. Now it seemed it was not only minutes they had left now to live – but seconds!

"Jab," Ricky spoke both honestly and nervously, "I love your hospitality with other creatures…."

"Thank you."

"…But this isn't the wild! You can't trust these guys!"

"Biff! These guys?" Jab said, very sure that these felines were no trouble. He knew if they were wolves, they would be dead already. "They invited us, plus they did rescue me and Apples."

"Sure, they did," Wallaba commented as he gave an unimpressed look.

"You guys need to know when it comes to gifts from other animals, its hospitality," Jab told them with knowledge. "It's rude to not take it. We must respect their rules and how they run the place. Then we can have a better understanding of each other's culture."

All the cats were heading inside as Jab gave a positive look at his friends. "This is going to be great, guys!"

The three rabbits stood still for a moment while the cats glared at them. "Shouldn't we tell him about

what's really going on?" Penny asked wondering
whether it would be wise.

"I don't think he knows." Ricky replied, "But I
do trust his instincts when it comes to meeting other
wildlife. Then, I would say we should follow him, till we
see any sort of trap ahead."

The rabbits journeyed inside the Cat House.

The rabbits entered the mansion and they saw
that the cats were all over it. It was like an old-fashioned
mansion but older, dusty and with too much fur. There
were cat enrichment toys and other things that helped the
cats to get themselves comfortable and entertained.

The cats themselves were mostly relaxed as they
had either high places or places on the carpet floor which
they chose as their restricted territory. They also played

with balls of strings that tied the place in knots, while others faced a toy mouse which drove a crowd to chase.

There were at least more than fifty cats in the house, but when they saw the rabbits enter their house, they didn't really do anything threatening. They all seemed to not be bothered.

While the rabbits watched where they were going - as most of them felt they should keep their distance - a few were arguing about Apples' latest retreat.

"But you ran off, man!" Wallaba told Apples in outrage. The other rabbits weren't impressed either. "We're here to keep a low profile and what do you do?!"

"Don't be mad at me." Apples pleaded. "Don't any of you think all of this is going rather too fast? Should we just take one step at a time?"

"Yeah, while we have only hours till our society falls apart!" Ricky told him they could not do things slowly; they didn't have a lot of time and time was running out fast.

Then, very unexpectedly, of all things, a small critter on roller blades came past the cats in every corner with no worries in the world. This was a ferret, who was the cats' personal servant.

The cats kidnapped him a while back, but he had no issue with them. He served the cats fresh milk because the roller blades would get him to get to places so easily. He liked the company here way more than he did with the other ferrets back home.

He spotted the uncommon guests and rolled over to them and bowed. "Jug Mi Ferret, at your service." he greeted them in a rich Spanish accent. It was quite a surprise for him to encounter animals other than cats, as all the other creatures he talked to in the last few months were cats.

The rabbits studied the animal quite narrowly, as they had seen creatures like Jug before, but not in the city.

"You're a ferret, right?" Ricky asked.

"That's exactly the question, isn't it?" the ferret said as he was playing words. He served the milk to the rabbits as if they would like to have some. "Have you had milk before?"

"No." Apples said as he took a glass of it. Penny thought bitterly that Apples shouldn't drink cat drinks. She slaps it out of his hand and the milk dropped.

"How do you know them so well?" Jab asked the ferret about the cats.

"Oh, yeah! they are excellent creatures!" the ferret said, who had many delightful memories about them. "They opened their arms and welcomed me."

"Did they try to kill you?" Ricky asked him as it was rather a personal question. He didn't mean to get things dark, but he needed to know for the safety of his friends.

"No. But they do have their moments. Sometimes." Jug couldn't remember a time when one of the cats tried to threaten him before. All of his memories were good ones in the house. He heard that other animals had issues with cats, but he just couldn't see it.

"You get to love it here, all the things these guys do," Jug said, as he faded into memory. "Boy, there were a lot of fun times."

"Have you left the Cat House?' Penny asked.

"Sometimes. Not all the time. These guys need my assistance, I can't leave them. We're best of pals."

Then the ferret's attention was cut short as he realised he should focus on his duties. "Sorry. Love to chat more, but I should see if there's a cat in need of my assistance." He drove off and waved at his rabbit friends as he did a little spurtle.

Jab had a quite positive thought about the critter as he seemed to like creatures like him. "He's quite nice."

"Well, he's an odd one," Ricky thought. He had never met a ferret but had heard stories about them. They built huts out of logs, lived in a pack, and went and showed all the other wildlife who was boss. But it seemed very odd for him to see one serving another species, and he didn't mind it.

"Well, I don't know what you all are on about," Jab told them as he couldn't imagine what they had been through. They walked through the hall past the cats.

A cat from above hissed as he tried to get their attention. The rabbits turned to hear what the cat was saying.

"There's a room for you on your left. Room service is a bit of a mess, but you all wouldn't notice a thing."

"Thanks," Jab said as he and the others headed off.

"Don't these guys seem very sus?" Wallaba asked the other rabbits as he couldn't shake the feeling.

"You and me bud," Apples told him. "I just can't pinpoint what I'm facing here." It was bothering Apples; he just hadn't seen a creature so confusing for him to identify, but the other rabbits knew more than he did.

10. The Attack!

It was morning sunrise at Tim Hole Village: the villagers picked out their crops and loaded them into town; a few rabbits played their own version of golf in the big open fields away from town; and a baseball tournament was held not so far away where the Wild Rickers and the Footers competed.

It was a nice summer day if you were not too dry or laying in a massive hot bath in the bathroom of the village; everything was all fine.

Two miles away from the village was the Military section which kept all their weapon resources and other supplies for the army. All the soldiers had been kept on guard so nothing would happen to them.

Rag gave them specific instructions that nothing must happen to them, and the area must be all secure and not to let anyone they didn't know in. It was only a matter of time and Rag knew Gabs may have one more trick up his sleeve before the battle began.

A few golfers were having a moment when they were swinging a nut over to a small hole - it didn't look like it was going to move. The poor fellow bunny was trying his hardest to swing it. That was until he noticed something was coming.

An unexpected army of red-armoured rabbits ridding chickens were charging into their territory with their carrot-jousting swords. The rabbit civilian sprung in surprise until he noticed he got poked many times by the riders and finally swung his nut in the wrong direction.

The chaos kept coming as they terrorised the villagers who panicked about what to do. The soldiers could see this from the military post. They argued that they couldn't let this happen, but they had clear instructions from their leader.

Later the riders put an innocent villager on a chicken and left him riding it as it was leading him to a travelling owl who did not expect to be attacked on his first day of travelling.

Mostly the attackers were only doing a small portion of destruction in the village. Their plan was only to try to get the soldiers away from the military base.

Part one of their plan wasn't going south, it was going north, but mostly it was going west. It was working, but the Tim Hole troops seemed to pull themselves together as Rag seemed to try to not lose the war. Rag knew if there was some kind of attack that it was meant to lure them out. He knew that was what his enemies wanted.

But there was another part of their plan. Every rabbit knew about the big match today. The last part of part one was to draw attention to the game - more and more attention!

There were chickens from Carrot Hill Sight, which wasn't too far off. A few of the attackers released a dozen chickens who ran out very astonished and headed towards the match.

The players, audience and the hosts were enjoying their time without knowing what had happened in the last five minutes. They soon spotted the chickens coming their way, and everyone thought they should get out of there.

"Oh my!" said one of the hosts. "It's some rogue wild chickens coming our way!"

As everyone left the stadium, no one knew what would happen when the chickens attacked. The chickens crashed and destroyed the entire stadium until it collapsed. Everyone moped that their game had come to a short end!

When the soldiers saw this at the military base, there was only rubble that remained of the stadium. But this droves them on the edge. They all enjoyed going to that stadium. Some of them even played there.

They didn't care what the attackers were going to do now; they destroyed rabbit property on purpose, and they were going to get it. One rabbit trooper out of the dozen took one foot out of the military line.

One other trooper stared at him. "What are you doing?" he said. "We're not supposed to be involved."

"I don't care!" snapped the soldier. "They have gone too far! I don't care what Lord Rag said, these rabbits must pay for their crimes!" He took out his carrot sword as he ran forward showing his true feelings. Then the other soldiers weren't entirely sure what to do any more, but they followed his lead and went into battle.

Jab and his pals had a good night's sleep without being terrorised by the cats next door. The cats gave them a room which they could have all by themselves with no interference. It was quite small and tall. Sunlight shone through the window over their area as they slept on a bunch of pillows, of which a few were torn off.

Apples was the first to wake up as he slowly opened his eyes until he saw the ferret right in his face.

"Wakey, wakey sleepy heads!" the ferret caught Apples in surprised shock, which woke everyone.

All the rabbits got up on their feet and rubbed their faces as they began their next move.

Jug followed them as they started to walk. "So, what are you doing now?" the ferret asked very generously but also with intrigue. "On the road? Seeing what the south side offers? My advice: don't drink human drinks, they have the strangest of juices."

"We're going to find a map." Jab informed the ferret. He knew informing wildlife was acceptable if they had an idea of where things were.

"A map?" the ferret asked the rabbit, "I know couple of places to find a map. One being in the main shopping centre."

"A what?" Ricky asked the ferret.

"Oh, it's full of humans. They go there all the time, walking about and going to visit places where they get stuff," the ferret informed them. "Such strange behaviour. But that's what you get when you know humans."

"We can't be anywhere near humans." Jab told Jug, as it was really important to keep the safety of his friends a priority and not let them be taken away. "Is there any other place nearby where we can find a map?"

"Yep, one," the ferret replied.

"Which that is…?" Penny asked.

"The shopping centre," said the ferret again. All the rabbits moaned. "Sorry, but I don't really go out in the city. You know how easy it is to get lost out there? And I don't want animal control on my radar."

"Us either," Jab thought as he sighed. He didn't think there could be any other way around it; he and the others only had less than twenty-four hours before the war would begin so time was ticking and precious.

"Do you think this 'shopping centre' is safe?" Ricky asked Jug.

"My opinion, no, not really. But if we were fast, maybe," the ferret replied; he seemed to be less helpful than he tried to be.

Ricky came over to Jab as they needed a moment together to figure out a plan. "Jab, you really think we should let this critter guide us to find this map?" Ricky asked importantly.

"It's worth a shot," Jab replied thinking he would give the critter a go.

"But we saw how dangerous this city is; can we trust him to look after us if he gave his word?"

Jab had a think about it. It was risky, but they got here this far, and they just about made at least one friend on the way. There was no guarantee, but you had to give trust to someone who knew his way around the place.

Jab looked back at Jug and told him, "Jug. Do you think you can keep an eye on us?"

"No guarantee," the ferret said as that was as far as he could be supportive.

Apples held up his paw up to draw Jab's attention. Jab gave Apples a focused look where he let Apples say, "Shouldn't we like get something to eat first?"

"Yeah, I'm feeling quite starving from all that traveling," Wallaba mentioned.

"Well then, I don't see why I should let you all go on an empty stomach," Jug told them, "I should know just the right place for a fine breakfast."

Near the Cat House was an ordinary human café where the rabbits and Jug made their way in from the back. They watched from below the chefs cooking up a steaming and warm bakery which reminded the rabbits of home already. Then an unusual smell took them by surprise, which Jug referred to as coffee.

The rabbits soon spotted humans at tables, enjoying their morning. Jug quickly stole few food items from the kitchen and took them outside to the rabbits.

What was on the menu were pasta with noodles, excellent egg and bacon, sausages, and a few grapes. They ate it all and enjoyed themselves for quite some time as they tried to savour the taste.

"That was…WOW!!" Penny said, having no word to describe it.

"Man, this place is the best!" Wallaba told himself without thinking about the dangers they had been through.

"Jug, how did you know you were a professional thief?" Ricky asked the ferret.

"Let's say I have few tricks up my sleeve other than what you may think of me!" the ferret commented, as he wished to not get into his past life. "Now, where exactly are you headed?"

"That's classified."

"Well, that's your business and I'm not going to get involved," Jug said, taking a bite out of a toast.

"What sort of dangers would you recommend that we should stay away from?" Ricky asked.

"Everything," the ferret said. "Mostly humans, but sometimes they're stupid and don't think straight, so it shouldn't be too much of an issue."

"Then what is the bigger danger?" Apples asked.

"Don't know. The world is a bizarre place. You may never know what you step your toes on."

The two armies clashed as Gabs' plan was piecing together. The smugglers were stealing some useful materials for their own as they drove outward from the village without being noticed.

Rag got out of his house as he and Yossi watched in horror and rage. The attack was getting out of hand as everything seemed to have gone sideways. But what drove Rag to his full anger was seeing his troops being involved even though he told them directly not to; he even wrote it on a paper for each of them and got them to memorize it.

"What are they doing?!?!" he roared.

"Uh…I think they are trying to fight off the attackers." Yossi replied, as he tried to lighten up Rag which wasn't going to be the case today.

"But I said no!" Rag was in a full temper as he saw this coming miles away. He was expecting an attack on the day before the war. He told himself that he wouldn't let himself be the fooled by a rabbit who could easily outsmart him.

Rag grabbed Yossi by his side as they walked through the town. All the things that lit the place were like a garage fire that had toilet paper thrown on it. The people just couldn't stop fighting one another as they couldn't tell what was happening anymore.

As much as this was outside Yossi's zone, he wasn't one of those cowards you see running from a fight or hiding away where no one would notice he was there. He wasn't a fighter either; you may describe him by saying he was just there without further things to add.

They came to a wounded soldier who was pinned down on the grass. The soldier looked at Rag and was caught by shock, "Lord Rag!"

"*Lord Rag*" mocked Rag. "Tell me what has happened here?!"

“Yeah, we were testing my brother for new clothes…” Yossi said as Rag pushed him out of the way.

The soldier had less than a word to describe the issue. He looked over to the battle and was trying to find some kind of excuses which either way was going to be very bad for him. “We saw the village under attack, and we thought we should go into action….”

“Without staying at the military base?!” Rag thought this was very extreme. “I told every single one of you to stay there if there was an attack!!!”

The soldier watched and witnessed the chaos he and the other soldiers had unfolded. He knew this was what Rag had feared may happen.

“Oooooooooooh.”

11. The Shopping Centre

The Rabbits walked through the street and noticed everything looked different. It wasn't as colourful as last night; everything seemed dull. And they spotted buildings that were so gigantic they couldn't see the top.

They finally arrived inside the shopping centre. It was a massively wide and large area where people were walking all about to different shops. The place went to four levels that the rabbits could see, and escalators were everywhere.

They came to the main centre - the food court – where people were sitting at tables. They also spotted big screens above them which changed into different images.

This was going to drive Apples nuts, but he was more calm than before. "This world does not make any sense" he had to tell the truth.

"You and me buddy." Wallaba commented, as he gave him a big pat on the back.

Penny was looking at a paper article on a table which caught her attention. She saw all these random topics that came out of nowhere, which gave little understanding to the rabbits. "I can't even read any of this. All of this just spangles my brain to even contemplate!"

"That's human talking there," Apples told her, "they just talk mumbo-jumbo wherever they go."

Jab was more focused on finding that map than to join in any small conversation. He followed Jug who tried to find a nearby map on a screen wall.

"There should be one that way," the ferret told Jab.

Jab nodded and turned his head around: only two rabbits were there. "Ah…" he said while looking around, "where's Wallaba and Penny?"

Apples gave a shrug which gave Jab the idea he wasn't trying his hardest effort.

Then there was a small patch of laughter and a bunch of gasps below them. The rabbits looked down and saw Penny was in a box of food; she was enjoying herself.

"Oh wow!" she said as she was eating the food, "this is way better than carrots! What is this stuff?!"

"Ah, I'll get her," Ricky said as he hopped carefully down towards her.

"What about Wallaba?!" Jab tried to call out to Ricky, but he was out of reach.

"Pss," called Apples behind Jab, "don't worry, I can go with Mr Ferret…."

"It's Mi Ferret to you," Jug corrected him.

"…while you go and find Wallaba."

"But that's the thing, Apples," Jab commented very dryly, "I don't know where Wallaba is."

Well, Wallaba had another thing he had been searching for his entire life. He wasn't sure what that was or if it was made up, but he found it. He came around to an arcade area where he found everything so engaging. If you were a small rabbit who was playing a thing like this, it would've taken hold of you even if you had a greater journey to make.

Humans normally played these games with their fingers and hand. For a rabbit, they tapped with their foot whenever the buttons needed to be hit. The people in the room saw how impressive the rabbit was, as he was beating their high scores. He was being much more than a bro.

Wallaba thought this was the best and most fun thing he had ever had. "Can you think you'll beat me like this?" he told the game. "I'll have more moves to play out." The high score was pretty high and the rabbit was surprised that no one tried to stop him.

Jab was calling out for him as he searched everywhere. He was lucky few people noticed him as he was being as stealthy as he could be. He shortly came to the arcade area where he saw Wallaba, which frightened him nervously.

He noticed that Wallaba was in a whole room full of arcade machines and humans, and a lot of people were surrounding him and cheering him on.

"Wallaba!!!!" Jab cried out.

"Jab, I'm busy," Wallaba called back.

"Busy?!" Jab said in shock, "you know we're on a mission?!!"

"Yeah, yeah, can you just wait till after I beat this thing?" Wallaba ignored Jab.

Jab knew nothing was going to stop him. Wallaba was smashing the buttons as if he was on fire; he had a purpose in life and he understood why.

Jab pounced on Wallaba which got him away from the machine which caused him to lose. All the crowed moaned in disappointment. Wallaba turned to Jab quite upset, "What the h…."

"Wallaba, we only have a few hours till war breaks; you can't just stay here while we're trying to prevent it!"

"Can't I?"

"No!"

Wallaba mumbled in silence as they hopped back to the others. They came over to a table where they bumped into Apples and Jug.

"We've done some research, and we know where to go." Apples reported.

"Excellent!" Jab thought thoughtfully. Then he froze. "Where's the others?"

Then a cry came from both Penny and Ricky. The three rabbits turned to see where it was coming from. They saw them trapped in a cage with two humans in uniforms, which told them they must be an animal rescue team. The three watched in horror as they saw their friends being taken away.

"Nonononono," Jab called, very scared that all his nightmares had arrived.

They hopped after them as Jug stayed behind and stood there very awkwardly. He knew he didn't want to be involved in any of these events as he would get the worse end of it.

"Well...that's it for me." he said.

The three rabbits hid in the parking lot where they watched the humans put their friends in a truck of some kind. They had the feeling it would be impossible to rescue them now.

"Our friends are in there!" Jab said without hesitating. "We gotta do something!!!" Jab tried to jump out, but Apples managed to pull him back.

"Jab, wait! We can't!" Apples said very logically.

"Are you kidding?! We can't let them take them! It won't be long till they get an emotional attachment with…with a human!!!" This horrified Jab. He thought the thing itself scared him enough, but if it was his friends, it was way more than he could bear.

He tried to resist Apple's grasp, but he couldn't do anything. "Jab, calm down!" Apples told him as he raised his voice. "We will get them out, but we have to plan how first."

"Exactly," Wallaba butted in. "I have an idea."

12. Rabbit Rescue

Jab, Apples and Wallaba sneakily jumped on board the truck laying down on the roof. It took about a twenty-minute drive until they arrived at the pet facility, where the truck drove downward to the basement.

The rabbits hid as they didn't want to be noticed by the animal handlers. They all watched as the handlers took their friends through a door which the three rabbits guessed would lead them further inside, but they still didn't want to be caught if anyone was around.

Wallaba noticed a vent above a shelf which could give them an easy access through the place. He touched his paw on Jab to get his full attention, but Apples was distracted.

They went to the vent and moved through a tight narrow tunnel which led them to different pathways. They could see the handlers under the vent taking their friends somewhere below. They noticed there were a few humans about, walking around the area. They came to a stop when one of the humans took their friends into a room that the vent didn't reach. It took about a minute until the man came out and locked the door with a key.

The rabbits had no idea what that small, yellow object was, but they knew they couldn't get in without it. They followed the man's trail as he led them to an office where he and another worker were chatting among themselves.

"Wanna go down there?" Wallaba asked Jab, taking the fall.

"Hey, let's not get so fast with conclusions here." Jab said, thinking that wouldn't be a good idea. "You two both did something stupid in the last forty hours, I don't see why I should take the blame."

"You have more experience." Apples replied.

Jab looked at them quite stunned. "The Retrieve have not done anything like this!"

"They will." Wallaba thought. He thought this was the sort of mission a member of the Rabbit Retrieve should go in for.

"Nah, Jab is right," Apples agreed with Jab's idea, "you take the leap!" he volunteered Wallaba, to which Wallaba felt quite betrayed.

"Me?! What about you?!"

"Me?!"

"Yeah," Jab agreed with Wallaba, "why shouldn't we chose you for the job?"

Apples tried to make an excuse, but he was terrible at excuses. "Oh, man!"

Jab and Wallaba headed back to where the truck was. They found a rope and pieces of string as they planned to get Apples down into the office stealthily, without any of the humans in the room spotting him. They lowered him down and Apples could see the key next to a computer drive. The handler was gone out of the room and the other human seemed to be getting some documents from a safe; his head was not paying attention to where Apples was.

The rabbits lowered him further, as slowly as could be. They couldn't tell if the man would notice anything. Apples came to the level where the key was, and he gave a nervous look for his pals to softly toss him over the side. They did as he indicated but they accidently slammed him into the computer drive. They quickly pulled him up when the human turned his head. As the human turned, he wasn't sure what happened but knew something was there for a moment.

The human was focused again on finding those documents, so the rabbits put Apples in the same position as before and he tried to reach for the key. The swing caused him to spin around, and he tried to get his grip on the key. But while he and his pals tried to get Apples back in position, the human walked back to the desk as he was about to have some lunch.

Apples froze as he tried to be some kind of prop. The guy stood there with his back to Apples, not sure what to do. The man turned as Apples grabbed his shirt from the back to hold on. When the man turned, he thought he could feel something. He turned around as Apples swung away and then hit him in the head which caused him to fall and drop unconscious.

Just then Apples' string broke which caused him to fall. "Auuuuugghh!!!!"

Jab and Wallaba watched on wondering where he went. "Apples?" Jab called out, hoping to find his friend.

Apples picked up the key and showed it to them. "Got it!!!"

Penny and Ricky were in a cage together when they spotted other rabbits in cages in a room full of them. They were stacked in shelves, and they could see everyone.

Penny and Ricky didn't know what may come next; they may never see each other again and feared the rest of their lives isolated with whatever owner they got. The thoughts consumed them as Ricky tried to bust open the bar, but nothing happened. "It's meant to open wide!" Ricky called.

"And how you know that?" Penny asked him.

"Because this sort of thing always does!"

As Ricky kept trying to open the cage, Penny had a nervous thought. She didn't want to be here in the human city if it wasn't for Jab's encouragement and doing what was right for their society.

"We need to get out of here!" she said.

"Get out of here?" said a mysterious but also quaky voice. It came from a rabbit on the other side who had black and grey fur and seemed to be having a rough time. "There's no getting out of here. Don't you young bunnies get it? When they catch you, there is no getting away."

"We got here by accident." Ricky explained thinking this rabbit should give Penny a break.

All the rabbits laughed hysterically as they thought Ricky just made a joke.

"How thick are you?" the rabbit teased.

"Hey!" Penny told them to shut up, "we came here to find Gum O'Rabbit!"

"He is in the city, being held hostage maybe." Ricky added.

"We came here to prevent a war which would end rabbit society as we know it." Penny continued.

"The least all you call can do - besides chuckling on being captured - is to shut up!"

When they spoke the name Gum O'Rabbit, every rabbit went quiet as they knew that this matter needed to be taken seriously. In spite of what these two had said, they were making fools of themselves.

"Whoopies!" said one rabbit.

"We have other friends on the outside." Penny explained. "They might help us."

"Might?" asked the rough rabbit. "You still don't have the clearest idea about how dangerous this city is, do ya?"

"We have experience." Ricky commented.

"Well, don't get your hopes high," the rabbit told them. "What will come out of those doors will be the rest of your lives!"

The three rabbits quickly exited the office without causing alarm. They hopped over to the corridor stealthily and hid and checked that nobody was coming. They sometimes leant against the walls as they moved along or rolled. Sometimes they hid in whatever decoration was nearby if they spotted a human standing or walking by. They soon came upon the door where their friends were kept.

"All right." Jab called pulling out the key. His friends lifted him and moved him towards the keyhole and Jab tried to turn it.

The plan was going quite well, until they could hear lots of footsteps coming.

Many footsteps were coming and caught the rabbits by surprise. They were in a tough situation in which they could not escape. They could either A: open the door anyway but the humans may grow suspicious and add three more bunnies on their adoption waiting list; or B: leave their friends behind and may or may not escape.

This wasn't a choice Jab could choose; he couldn't choose anything like that. This drove Apples to act.

"I'll distract them," he said quite confident.

"What?! You're crazy?!" Wallaba told him.

"Look, I can go for a nice chase with these guys while you get the others out - deal?" Apples' attitude seemed so positive, but Jab couldn't go with it. "I'll make it easy for you!"

Apples jumped off and rushed towards the humans. Jab luckily was still on the keyhole and tried to turn it. Apples came upon a lot of humans and sat nicely until everyone just stopped and looked at him.

"Who's going to stop me?!" Apples told them.

The humans chased down Apples which drove them in a different direction away from Jab and Wallaba. They could hear people yelling as they were chasing Apples, and Jab finally got the door to open.

Jab and Wallaba got into the room where they spotted Penny and Ricky among the other rabbits.

"Jab! Wallaba!" Ricky and Penny called out in excitement.

Jab and Wallaba jumped onto their cage. "I thought I didn't keep you long," Jab commented, "besides, we've got a busier day ahead of us."

Then Penny noticed, "Where's Apples?"

"He thought he could drive the humans away."

"But don't worry," Wallaba finished. "I have a feeling he will be able to outrun them."

They took a closer look at the cage which seemed impossible to unlock. "This looks tough."

"I told you; you won't be able to escape!" the rabbit on the other side commented.

"Yeah, I get that," Jab replied, ignoring him.

"I tried to bust the bars but guess what?" Ricky asked Jab.

Jab tried to open it, but he noticed this was one carrot that he couldn't open. "This isn't looking good."

"Allow me." Wallaba offered as he was bigger. His paws gripped the bars and shortly flicked the cage open.

"Good job!" Penny complemented him as she and Ricky walked out. "Now, how do we get out of here?"

Then a tap came from the window from the far corner which they didn't spot before. Outside was that grey cat from last night who got their attention.

"There's an exit near the right side, you won't miss it. Meet me near the lake." The cat vanished as the rabbits did the same.

The four bunnies made their leave as Jab remembered one other thing. He looked back to the other caged rabbits and asked them, "Shall I release you all?"

The rabbits had a think about it. "Nah", they all replied as they all agreed, "we want to have a quieter life and see what's next for us."

Jab wondered why, but he didn't really argue. "Suit yourself!" he said as he and his pals took their leave. The caged rabbits were happy in their comfortable lives as they weren't planning to be rescued; they thought they should spend their days in a new human home and…what?

…they haven't thought this through. Maybe that opportunity was gone, and they should have taken it while they had the chance. Oh well.

13. Final Hour

Jab and his pals followed the instructions the cat had told them. They escaped outside to a very quiet alleyway that led to a street. But all the rabbits were curious about Apple's whereabouts, worried that it must have drawn a lot of people's attention to chase one rabbit.

But as they finally took a rough stop, Jab had a shocking revelation as he stared out to the sky.

"It's afternoon!" he said, quite surprised and also quite nervous. "But it can't be afternoon!"

"Well, time does go by when you're going all over the place," Wallaba thought.

Jab couldn't accept it. War would break tomorrow, and they just wasted an entire day. He couldn't let every single rabbit down, including the next generation of their kind.

"We must get to Gum!" Jab said, as he started to race off.

"Jab! Where are you going?!" Ricky called to him as he tried to catch up.

"We can't let this war break out! We just can't!" Jab told him with his heart bouncing.

"Jab, wait!" Ricky told him. He tried to get his friend to slow down for one moment. "There's nothing we can do now, but we can still get to him."

"Which is why I have to go!" Jab told Ricky and gave him and his friends a sorry expression. He went off and passed to the next street until Ricky was out of sight.

Ricky and the others arrived at a lake where they gazed out over the city as the sun set. Boats and ferries floated in different directions, and buildings and towers rose on the other side.

The rabbits talked about what Jab did for the last two days hoping it was making a difference, hoping to change something terrible into a spark of hope. They all had negative experiences in the human city, but it was all for a cause. But was it? But now Jab was gone, out of reach and contact and they had little clue as to where he was now.

Shortly after, Apples caught up with them. It seemed he had to rush.

"Hey guys!" he called to them, quite overwhelmed. "Where's Jab?"

The rabbits looked very miserable, and they didn't turn around.

"Don't know," Ricky replied dimly. "He just left us."

"Just like that?" Apples asked. "That doesn't sound like him. Where do you think he has gone?"

"Who even knows?" Penny told him.

"That's it." Wallaba thought. "We failed."

The rabbits wanted to say no, but Wallaba was right - it was far too late. Hopping around the city while they lost their main objective on many occasions. Now they wondered where Jab was.

"Yeah, but Jab made a change," Ricky told his pals. "He wouldn't accept that, and neither should we!"

"Yeah!" they all thought brightly.

"And he wanted us to follow him," Ricky went on. "Why would we be here except because of him?"

They all stared and wondered. Yeah, he did make a change. Jab had his friends would go on this wild journey, even if it was already too late; Jab encouraged them to the very end.

"We all trusted him, no matter how impossible this task was. And now he has gone off in this strange city and we're just…"

Then they stopped as Ricky looked over to a pizzeria where the grey cat was laying on a table. He looked like he was enjoying himself today. He made a yawn which stopped Ricky talking.

The rabbits went up to him. The cat seemed to be relaxing until he noticed them. He rose his eyes as he greeted them. "Weeelll, isn't this a surprise?" he said quite happy.

The rabbits looked at him in confusion.

"Why are you here?" Wallaba asked him.

"Are you trying to follow us?" Apples questioned him, as he still did not fully trust him.

"Why would I bother my whole day following you guys?" the cat asked, as it seemed not to be his style. "I could, if I wanted to."

"Then, why?" Penny asked. It seemed to be a big jump to reach here from where they last met.

"Destiny, I suppose," the cat said, as he ignored them. Then he caught his eyes on the remaining pizza he was eating. He passed them a slice of pizza as he wanted to be nice. "Wanna taste this?"

The rabbits looked at each other as they weren't sure if they wanted to eat it. Besides, they did have a horrible day.

"It's quite delicious," the cat told them, and he wasn't lying.

They hopped on board one of the ferries, acting quite different. After they ate the delicious slice, they had the imagination of wonder, of something new. They travelled all over the ship trying to find something else delicious to eat.

Ricky and the cat stayed put and spent time together. Ricky needed it because of what he had been through, and he knew the others were more capable of looking after themselves.

"That was so good," Ricky said as he remembered the taste of the pizza and that feeling of a new experience that wouldn't go away.

"You and me, buddy," the cat replied. He was welcoming to anyone, including non-cat-like animals. He was as chilled as before. Ricky guessed he wasn't much of a threat.

"You're not quite so imposing as I had thought," Ricky said. "Why?"

The cat was busy in the middle of a dream until he shook it off. He liked the company more than not having anyone talking to him; he thought he might explain why.

"Well. I thought me and the other cats were just street thugs who imposed on any critter that came into our neighbourhood. But since you guys arrived, I thought, what's even the point anymore."

Ricky gave both a worried look but somehow relaxed look, and the cat continued, "Anyway, cats normally don't cope seeing anyone. But you just seem to interest me."

"How so?" Ricky asked.

But the cat had just one thought. "Don't know. You seem so encouraging. We…we don't have that." He looked at Ricky who seemed to have changed his view on the world. "Maybe I should have helped you all this time besides being in the background."

Ricky enjoyed this conversation with the cat, but his mind was now focused on the war, which would begin tomorrow.

"War is about to begin tomorrow." he told the cat very seriously.

The cat seemed to be pretty understanding but wasn't aware of such events occurring. "Ah," he said, "look, we cats don't bother into politics, but from what I've seen, you guys do."

Even though it was hard to judge, Ricky had to agree with this. He nodded.

"But that's the sort of thing we stay away from," the cat explained. "Why do you think we don't care all the time? We do care sometimes, but we know if we start to begin a revolution it might destroy us."

And with that, Ricky feared - was everything that the rabbit society was built on a mistake? Have they become the new humans?

"I..I never wanted to go through with this," Ricky explained. "This war has torn apart our world. And the reason why I joined Jab on this quest was so I could stop it too. Before it was too late.”

The cat looked at Ricky and saw how much he was struggling, knowing hopes were lost and there was nothing to go back to at home. Which made the cat consider, “Alright, I’ll help you find your friend if I can.”

“You can?” Ricky asked him if it was worth the trouble.

“Hey, war’s breaking out tomorrow, and here’s you saying you think all hopes are over. You know how much that makes me sick?”

“How much?” Ricky wondered.

Then the cat pauses, “Not as much as having too many litres of milk,” he thought. “But that isn’t the case. I’m going to help you!”

The ferry passed under a bridge as a new dawn began.

When the battle ended, everything was mostly back to normal, except that the stadium was now completely in ruins, and their mayor was gone away to have an urgent meeting with Gabs.

Rag took an emergency ride to Carrot Hill Sight Village. He rode an owl that flew him towards the village. But at Carrot Hill Sight, Gabs was happily at his own home with nothing else but tea to have to spend the rest of the day. He had Perm over to be in service. They were waiting for the return of the team with their new supplies. They would soon plan how to use them in the upcoming battle.

Then Perm thought, "You know what, that was a good plan."

Gabs took a slurp from his tea as he added, "It's about phases. You need to add one idea to it before you can extend it and then execute your goal."

"Well, one out of three, isn't so bad." Perm refered to the other rabbits' plans.

There wasn't a knock that altered their moment together; it was more like a dramatic slam as the door opened. Rag was caught by two bodyguards holding him before he could take one step inside.

"You stole my stuff!!!!" the outraged leader yelled.

This visit surprised Gabs and Perm as it was unexpected; they weren't going to see Rag again till the war, but it looked like plans were changing by the minute nowadays.

But Gabs should have expected that Rag was going to do something like this. It would have given more of a worrying feeling if Rag had pushed himself to these limits to get here and stumbled into Gabs' domain without any notice. If that would draw Gabs to conclude he should put Rag in prison. But in fact, rabbits don't really commit any sort of crime so there was no real point to having a prison, which made Gab's choice more simple, "Let him in."

The bodyguards took him in a few feet while they still grabbed his arms. They let him go when Rag shoved them off.

"You really think you could get away with it so easily, am I right?" Rag forcibly teased the other leader who shared no compassion. "Would you go that far to claim it all? You should have decided to be ruler when we had the chance."

"We had that chance, but you backed down," Gabs told him.

"Me back down?!" Rag said so shocked and knew he had about enough of Gab's nonsense. "I told you there was no way around this, and you said no! but there was one, wasn't there?"

Gabs looked intensely. He went quiet. Rag knew he was putting him on the spot. "You knew if you could tangle me and all my friends up, you would get your way anyway, and there's no war, there's not even something I'm competing with here. It's just you, and it will always be you. Because one day, someone will back away from you because they know their ruler is nothing but a dictator who wants nothing but to be on top of everyone else!"

Rag looked over to Perm's expression, sharing the emotion of both shame and disappointment. "You think I'm all bad? I'm the one who has problems?" then he looks at Gabs miserably, "he's the one you all should worry about!" Rag marched out of the house and the bodyguards followed him.

Even though it was a short and unexpected visit, Gabs knew exactly why Rag had come. To put him off his plans, to lose trust, to think he will lose it, and he would lie to himself time and time again, even to his village, maybe soon, his entire species, even Gum O' Rabbit.

Perm looked at Gabs with an emotion he never shared with his friend before. He never liked it, but he was scared of what his leader had become.

"Gabs," he said softly and firmly. "What have you done?"

The rabbit leader grew even more silent than ever. He replied by a fearsome terminating glare at Perm, "It all begins tomorrow," he said. "Tomorrow the rabbit rebellion shall commence!"

14. It Begins

It was five o'clock in the morning. The streets of Brookland were quiet and steady. Few cars passed and a few humans decided to take a very early jog if they didn't feel weird getting up so early. But they were all aware of what was happening.

An army of rabbits in leather battle armour, riding on chickens and welding carrot-jousting sticks were marching in the street. They were lined together like a pack of lined-up toy soldiers. It wasn't the humans' imagination; it was really happening.

The humans couldn't tell what was going on. They wanted to film them, but they just couldn't as the situation seemed so bizarre.

Even aware of the dangers in the human city, the rabbits ignored them as this was a different story. The rabbits wanted to show the human race what they were capable of and to warn humans to not mess with them.

"HOLD!" said the lieutenant who was in front of the line. Most of the rabbits in the front banged into each other as they were forced to stop. The lieutenant sniffed and stared at the road. The concrete seemed old, rough, and very easy to see the cracks underneath. But something was off about it.

Rabbits have many different skills; one may be very fast, another could tap a glass very quickly until it shattered, or one like him could easily trace stuff.

The tracer can identify and sense what moved here in the last two hours. The lieutenant was really good at tracking, and he knew the tracing seemed obvious and familiar. "Rabbits were here." he said, as he knew the enemy was not far.

"Rabbit tracks?" asked one of the troops while all of them stood in wonder.

"Sir?" asked one bunny who was in a far corner near the end of the line. "How can you tell its rabbit tracks?"

"Pardon?" said the lieutenant who could only hear the last word.

"How can you tell its rabbit tracks?"

The lieutenant had trouble hearing him. "Hey, can you come over to me, passing all the others and stay in the third front row?" Then the lieutenant looked at another rabbit in the line. "You! Take his spot!"

The rabbit came to him slowly as he excused everyone he passed by. But the rabbit was dopey and dim-witted as this rabbit had no sense of training or being here. This was Yossi we're talking about.

He decided to join the battle, but he didn't ask his brother for permission to be here. But he thought he would join the good fight.

"Right!" the lieutenant said, who had no knowledge who this bunny was. "What did you say?"

"I SAID HOW CAN YOU TELL ITS RABBIT TRACKS?!" Yossi yelled out, much closer to be heard.

"I have skill," the lieutenant explained, as he rolled his eyes towards the roof tops as if some kind of ambush was waiting to happen, and they were just walking right into it. He could nearly see some rabbits hiding through a window on the third level which might be an abandoned building.

This rabbit had ideas and knowledge of when these sorts of attacks may occur and how best to avoid them. "We will go around, and try to find another way."

"Fantastic idea!" Yossi complimented him and later shut it. He told himself to shut it as that's what commanders would say. That's why the army never let him in as he would get on everyone's nerves.

Ricky and the others woke up and noticed the Ferry had finally arrived at a stop. They also noticed the sun was up and it gave them a bad impression. They were all scrumpled together as they looked at the morning sky.

"War is here," Penny thought very dimly.

But that didn't stop Ricky though. "All right, war is here, I get that. But we cannot leave Jab here in this city."

"Yeah, but how are we supposed to find him?" Apples wondered.

"That's why Lanord will help."

"Lanord?" the other rabbits wondered. They guessed who that was, then they looked at the cat who was with them.

"He said he has contacts all around the city," Ricky explained. "He can reach out to other cats from far distances to ask if they could find a little rabbit hopping around, having little clue where he was going. And then they would bring him back to us."

Lanord gave a little optimistic look as he tried to state a negative. "That depends really," he said, "They may eat him on the spot."

The rabbits looked horrified as they thought not to cross that thought again. "And if we can't find him with Gum O' Rabbit, we'll go home."

The rabbits felt that if they did that, everything would be pointless being here. But they had to agree with Ricky on this one: they had to find Jab and that's what they will do.

"It's a pretty good plan," Penny thought.

"Then, let's go find Jab," Wallaba commented as the rabbits began their search for their lost friend.

Jab kept moving through the night and day, wasn't stopping until he reached Gum O' Rabbit. He forgot that his pals had the address, and he never knew what it was.

He kept moving no matter how tired he was; he started to lose his sense of time as he couldn't tell if it was morning or noon. He started to take a breather as he rethought what he was doing.

He came to an alleyway where it seemed quite quiet in this area, but he was still in the city. He paused while he tried to rethink himself.

"What am I doing?" he asked himself quite tiredly.

He left his friends behind, dragged them on this wild quest and put them in danger more times than he could remember. Not only that, but he was trying to prevent the inevitable. Even though Jab knew that this war must be prevented, he started to learn that it was getting the better of him.

Jab was the sort of rabbit who wanted to help animals and rabbits in all places, not the sort who would enter into dangerous territory and risk losing his friends in the process.

And also he did a jerk thing by leaving his pals behind. What would the Retrieve think of him now? Leaving a member behind?

As Jab nearly started to lose hope, he froze as he saw a cat coming out of a cat door, going to go for an ordinary walk. Then he noticed Jab. He wasn't trying to be terminating but was rather quite scared by the rabbit.

Jab gave an aggrieved look at the cat as he had had enough trouble already. The cat feared that he was going to mug him, but he didn't have anything to take.

The cat backed away as he tried to enter back inside.

"Hey, hey, hey!" Jab called out as he quickly pulled the cat back. Jab caught him at the cat door and gripped onto his head.

The cat's eyes were wide in terror as he saw the full terror in the rabbit's eyes.

"Please!" the cat pleaded. "Let me go! I don't want to be part of anything!"

"TELL. ME. WHERE. IS. GUM. O. RABBIT!" Jab warned him as he tried to force the information.

"No, no rabbit here, man!" the cat giggled nervously. "Seriously, I don't know any rabbit! I haven't eaten a bird because I thought it would be good, or annoyed my owner by spilling his coffee on himself, I was just wanted to be good!"

Before Jab could interrogate further, he noticed that he may have stepped over the limits. He started to restrain himself as he said calmy. "I'm sorry about this. I just had a rough couple of days."

"I imagine everyone has a rough couple of days around here," the cat agreed as he tried to get back inside but couldn't.

"It's just that I am trying to stop this bad thing that is happening. All rabbit-kind will soon be destroyed if I can't find our leader."

"Ah-huh."

"But my friends, I left them behind."

"You must be a terrible friend. Don't worry, I left my friends a number of times. But they knew I was a kinda bad influence."

"And my friends may think the exact same thing." Jab froze for a moment while the cat had no idea what he was doing.

"Hey, I might go inside, cool?" asked the cat.

"Listen," Jab told the cat to focus. "I only want to know where I can find him, and the only way I can is if

you know where. So, where's Second Three Don
Avenue?"

"Second Three Don Avenue?" the cat said, who
seemed to know the name. "It's just around the block.
Well, not from this area, but over two blocks away."

"Really?" Jab said quite hopeful.

"Yeah, just go there and be on your way."

"No, you're taking me there."

"WHAT?!" the cat said quite shocked. "But…but
I told you the way. Isn't there any other guidance I could
give you?"

"I need to be sure," Jab told the cat. "I've been
all over the place yesterday and now I'm not going to be
lost again."

The cat gave a very scared look as he just wanted
to stay put, be a good cat. But he knew he wasn't going
to be sorry for the rabbit.

The rabbit army from Tim Hole Village kept on the move as they passed through the street and noticed there were multiple ambushes waiting to happen, but they tried to not step into any of them.

Yossi started to understand why Rag hated Gabs, as he always had clever and cunning plans. Even as their success was grim, he didn't mind. "They seem to be well organised," Yossi told the lieutenant. "I wonder if my brother…I mean, our soon-to-be ruler should have thought of some clever plans like this."

"They appear to be in every section of the city," the lieutenant noticed. "We have to stay strong if we want to win this."

They came to another spot on the street where they spotted another troop coming. It was the troopers from Carrot Hill Sight Village emerging. They didn't seem to be in larger numbers than at Tim Hole Village.

"Yikes," Yossi thought, "they look just like us! If you can imagine that."

"But they're not us," the lieutenant thought.

One of the soldiers at the front looked back at Yossi and asked him, "Here, take my place."

"Sure," Yossi replied happily, as the soldier went in back in the line. Then the other rabbits did the same as they asked Yossi to take their place and Yossi happily agreed, until he was standing next to the lieutenant.

The lieutenant looked at him quite startled and surprised. "Where did you come from?" he asked.

"I'm not sure," Yossi replied. "What's the plan?"

"There's only one course of action to take if our enemy has a full advantage on us," the lieutenant said as he stared into the gaze of his enemies. "SCATTER! SCATTER!"

All the rabbits did so, but that's when everything went wrong. The ambushers jumped and pounced onto them as they landed. Everyone drew out their jousting carrots as the two armies clashed.

Shortly after, each fell as their sticks hit each other. Some waved theirs to try to take down as many of their enemies as possible, which was quite a good technique.

Others ran while waving about, having no idea what to do. A few were on their chickens as they went wild and lost control over them. Others lay traps and caught their enemies quite easily.

Yossi looked down at a button that fell off his armour. He thought he should pick it up as he needed all the protection he could get. Until one of the jousting carrots wacked him on the back which made him fall on the ground. "OW!" he called. "No fair."

The groups later scattered across the street as they all fought. That was the thing about scattering - it wasn't that the leader was trying to act dumb, they needed to scatter their men about so they could have a better advantage. Was it a bad idea? Who really knew because nobody cared for it.

15. Save or Change the Future

Ricky and the others journeyed through the city in their search for Jab. Lanord tried to call out to nearby cats about any rabbit sightings, but there wasn't any luck. "Got nothing," he replied to the rabbits as they walked.

"He has to be somewhere," Ricky commented.

They journeyed towards an alleyway which was narrow with brick walls and led to different pathways.

On the corner on the right-side, something sprang at them – rabbits that were ninja-like, armoured samurai assassins! They stared at the rabbits tensely while holding carrot swords.

Ricky and the others froze as they tried to not make any movement, not even a sound. The assassins were also quite still, thinking that they would attack quite suddenly.

"On my mark," Ricky whispered to his pack.

"What?" Apples asked loudly, causing the assassins to charge. The rabbits ran!

The rabbits ran on foot as the assassins jumped on the brick walls and bounced off. The rabbits kept their speed as they found a nearby door opening where a human in white clothing came out.

As the rabbits entered inside, they ran into a kitchen where the chefs watched in both confusion and horror. The assassins hopped over the kitchen's ovens and fire pans as they clawed their way to the rabbits. The rabbits looked back and saw them catching up to their tails.

The rabbits found an exit which they tried to push open. "Hurry, hurry!" Penny told Wallaba.

"Human doors are much heavier than they look!" he told her.

The assassins threw their carrot daggers, and the rabbits knew they were out of time. Apples and Ricky pushed open the door. They all stepped outside, then closed it.

They heard few thuds on the door and thought they might have had it. Then they got a tap on their backs. They turned around quite frightful, but it was Lanord, "You guys are very jumpy, you know that?"

He asked the rabbits if they wanted to ride on his back. They jumped on as the cat jumped on to a nearby wall and walked stealthily.

Not so far away, they spotted their assassins on the way to block their path. Lanord leapt off the wall and rushed through another alleyway where they could hear a busy road near ahead.

Then two assassins rammed Lanord which bounced all the rabbits off him. They turned to look at their feline friend, but he was busy tackling them on the ground.

"You guys go!" he told the rabbits. "I can at least hold them off for a little while."

The rabbits didn't want to leave him behind, but they saw more assassins still coming, so they kept on moving.

The cat led Jab to his Ruler while they walked through the street. They climbed over a ladder leading to a balcony, but they kept going. They arrived at the fourth floor up and walked over through a small column near the window side. They tried to keep on their guard. The cat pointed out a window on the other side of an apartment where Gum was.

"There," the cat pointed over to the building. "He is over in that room there in that exact same window…"

"Thank you," Jab replied. "Look, sorry for threatening you, it…"

Then Jab noticed as he looked back to the cat, the cat tried to swipe the rabbit which caused Jab to nearly fall, if it wasn't for him holding his grip on to the column.

"What are you doing?!" Jab asked the cat both confused and terrified.

"What are you doing?!" the cat replied back, with the exact same emotions. He tried to stomp his paws on the rabbit's paws, but Jab still managed to hold on. "Why isn't he dropping?!"

"Why are you trying to kill me?!"

"Why wouldn't we?!" the cat told him, as it sounded like the kind of thing they would do. "You're our playthings, our prey. I hate being one of them you know, but I can't just help it."

"Don't you want to save rabbit-kind?" Jab asked if that was what the cat wanted.

"Nope!" the cat responded, as his tapped his paws again and Jab fell. Jab was caught on a thin string which was tied by clothing he held on to.

The cat watched from a distance and was quite surprised about how this little rabbit was still able to hold on to his precious life.

Jab held on till he heard a snap on one side which caused him to swing over to the other apartment.

As Jab hit to one of the windows; he smacked onto it then he slowly slid down. But when Jab tried to get his vision back again, he noticed in the corner of his eye on the other side of the interior room was an old rabbit in a small cage on a desk.

Jab flicked his eyes to see if they were trying to play any games. It was! Gum O' Rabbit! Sleeping in a cage. "Gum!" Jab tried to call out while continually tapping on the window.

Gum paid no attention and was not aware of Jab. He must have been taking a full-on deep sleep. Jab spotted on the window was some sort of metal needle in it; he pulled it and the window flooded up. Jab got into the apartment.

Jab got up to the desk where Gum was and opened the cage for Gum's freedom. "Gum, thank god I found you!"

"Hmm?" the old leader spoke as his eyes rose. He looked at the young bunny. "Oh!"

"Come on!" Jab told him as he raced back to the window. "We gotta race back to the village!"

"Village?"

"Yeah, whatever you chose. Anyway, we gotta tell them about your absence."

"I don't think I will be going."

Jab stopped and froze, then slowly turned back to the ruler. "What?"

"I grew so much to like this place," the leader commented. "I was walking through the fields you see, and my owner…"

"Owner?!" Jab stopped Gum as he spoke, more shocked. "Gum, tell me they didn't get to you!"

"Yeah, his a nice man, you see. He gives me a good meal, good floor, good…"

"Stop! Stop!" Jab told him, as he wasn't sure how much longer he could take it. "Gum, this is what happens when you get so close to the human colony. You get used to them, lose your free will. You're the wisest rabbit we ever knew."

"It's not bad as you may think, if only you get to know them better."

"And I cannot believe I'm hearing this!" Jab rubbed his head and tried to figure out what to do. Their ruler has been completely brain washed and lost his understanding of his duties.

Gum stared at him with a typical look. "Young bunny," he spoke normally. Jab knew this sounded like their leader even if he wasn't the same before. "My time as ruler has finally come to an end."

Jab gave the Ruler a look of astonishment. "Don't you see why I've come here?" he told him, his tone intense. "There's a war going on, and the only way to stop it is if you come back."

"Well, they just have to get used to it," Gum said as it sounded unfair.

"But if…, why aren't you listening to me?!"

"Because it's my breakfast time," Gum said, as he headed back into his cage and ate his meal inside.

Jab watched his leader eating like he was some kind of pet; he would never understand why rabbits would behave like this. "But you have to convince them to stop," Jab told the ruler as he had to fix this. "Rag and Gabs aren't going to make any agreement and you know deep down it will never happen."

Gum finished cowing his meal as he swallowed it in and took a moment to breathe and answer. "Young bunny, I'm not going to be the rabbit who's going to be there all the time," he said wisely. "How old am I?"

"About forty-eight years old," Jabs said with knowledge. "You're kinda immortal."

"No, kid. You need to face reality," he told him to get his head straight. He felt he should get all his rabbits heads straight on this matter. "Rabbits must work out how to get along with each other, no matter how stupid they are, they have to."

Jab paused and looked down as he thought, "But how can I gain all of your wisdom to pass on?" Jab asked. He wasn't sure how do that; he was young and just a new recruit of the Rabbit Retrieve, no one would ever listen to him, especially not Rag and Gabs.

Gum tilted as he came over to the young bunny.

"Tell me," he asked with interest. "Why did you come here?" Jab looked at him. "What made you decide to take all this effort just for me to fix it?"

Jab thought of his next words wisely while Gum told him not to make a fool of himself. "I wanted to help, that's all I wanted."

"Then do something," Gum told him. "Even if it is impossible, do something you won't regret. Be that spark that will save our rabbit kind!"

16. Ending a War

The rabbits made their way to an abandoned factory which was totally deserted, but it didn't stop their assassin friends from following. The rabbits looked back and saw that they were gaining on them; it seemed like their feline friend wasn't much of a fighter.

The assassins flew a bunch of their carrots at them, but the rabbits dodged, and they hit the iron pylons.

Ricky was having a hard time getting away from them and turned. One of the assassins backflipped in front of Ricky as Ricky dropped on his back. Wallaba and Penny came to his aid as few of the assassins cornered them.

"For our greatest ruler who ever lived!" one of the assassins spoke out. "RAG!!!!"

"RAG!!!!" the rest of the assassins called out.

"Him?!" Ricky said very unimpressed. "He is no ruler; he is just a clown!"

"Speak of his name like that again, and we will do what we must!" the assassin warned, pointing his carrot sword at them as the rest drew closer.

Then they noticed above them was a giant pot coming down and they all had one thought of action: spread out! They all moved away as they jumped on tables and chains as liquid was pouring on the ground.

Ricky and the others ran to find stairs leading out. Apples soon joined them as he was the one who dropped the pot. "I think I should have an apology!"

"Not now!" Ricky told him as he could see the assassins were making their way toward them again. They headed out onto the streets.

The army started to bring cannons with big noodle balls inside to hit their target as their enemies got stuck in the noodles. The battle grew even more intense as the humans watched and weren't sure what to do. They just had to ignore them and go on with their own business.

The battle headed into the alleyways, rooftops, and interiors of the abandoned warehouses where it drew less attention from the human population, but these were also places where no one could escape. Others went to lower grounds, hoping to hide and strike.

Yossi had no idea what he was doing; he went over to look for a fellow rabbit as he hoped he could be part of a pack again.

The rabbits headed up on the rooftops as others tried to stay there and hopefully not fall off.

Chicken riders charged into their opponents as they rolled like bowling pins but rolled for quite a distance.

Yossi ducked as he thought the best strategy he could have was to lay low. He spotted a few rabbits hiding under the sewers thinking they didn't want any attention. "Hey! Can I chill you with guys?!" he asked nicely.

"No, go away!" they said. "You'll spoil our location!"

Elsewhere, a group of rabbits were in a tight corner as their enemies were clashing through and they weren't sure how far they could keep going. This war may just end by afternoon.

From a pigeon's view: he could see a giant battle taking place over at a corner where bits of the street seemed very discarded so that no cars drove there. But on the way, he could see a few rabbits being chased through a human pathway on the street where rabbit-like assassins were chasing them.

They had to pass humans, tables, and other things when they were running. Every time they looked back, the assassins were there!

Then the rabbits saw a taxi driving by as they raced onto the road and just managed to grip onto it. They held on to the bottom as they tried to get up.

They looked back. The assassins were keeping up as they were much stronger. The young rabbits pulled themselves up and leapt onto the top, but the taxi used its breaks suddenly causing the rabbits to fly off.

They landed on the ground and saw their chasers weren't done yet. They later found a man pushing a trolly which got hijacked by the rabbits.

"This is unbelievable!" Wallaba cried out as he wasn't sure he could keep doing this.

They saw the assassins had jumped onto the bottom of the trolly as it swung across. It swung back to the road which luckily managed to escape from a car.

"These guys are like, well trained!" Apples noticed as they still tried to shake them off.

"Don't they know who's side we are on?" Penny wondered. "Or are they the kind to attack on sight?"

"Penny, I don't want to know," Ricky told her. Ricky shortly noticed that one of the assassins came near her and he was about to swing his carrot at her. Ricky quickly shoved the weapon and pushed the guy off.

Then one of the assassins finally managed to climb up the trolly and jumped onto Wallaba who struggled to move.

"Get off me!" Wallaba roared as he shoved him off and saw him flying.

The rabbits tried to see what they could do but everything was out of control; the trolly was moving and spinning and they were losing track of the assassins. The trolly spung around and avoided cars at the last second.

That's until three of the assassins popped up as they cornered the rabbits. The assassins were about to finish the young rabbits until a jug of milk was thrown at two of them, and the third was pulled away. A very familiar face returned.

"I think this is my ride," Jab said as he got the assassin off.

The rabbits cheered and were very relieved to see their friend again. "Jab!"

"Ah, hey guys," he replied. It seemed a while since they last met each other.

But someone was paying attention to the traffic when no one else was.

"Watch out!" Apples yelled out as the trolly hit the tip of the pathway, causing everyone, including the shopping, to fly to the ground.

A bucket hit Wallaba and a bunch of fruit hit Apples on the head. Everyone was trying to gain consciousness as they got up.

"That…was heart bounding," Ricky thought.

"Yeah," Jab agreed. "Maybe we won't do that again."

They took notice and saw near them was the battle unfolding. The rabbits going out there started to lose their understanding. It was quite a sad experience as they looked at the mess they caused, and chickens wondered around with little sense of what was going on.

As they watched this, they came to realisation: was this all necessary? They knew they needed a Ruler, but did they really have to fight over it? It didn't clear these soldiers' thoughts and there was no need for victory. At the end, it was pathetic, just pathetic stuff!

Jab turned back to his friends who gave a guilty look.

"Look guys," Jab began, "I'm sorry that I brought you guys into all of this."

"Don't be," Penny replied happily.

"You wanted to make a difference," Wallaba told him to cheer up.

"We wanted to come along because you needed help," Ricky told him. "Even if the whole city is a mess and there's chickens running about, we're still your friends."

Jab slowly made a small smile.

"Thank you," he said, quite astonished about how far they had come. He really couldn't have gone far without them. They all came to a huddle into a massive hug which caught Jab off guard.

Then, on a rubble of mess rose their Ruler, Gum O' Rabbit, who sensed the disappointment of all rabbits he saw in front of him. The soldiers shortly paused as

they saw him: one by one they froze as they noticed
there was no need for more fighting.

Gum stared at all the troops and gazed over the
dim afternoon.

"Hmm," he said quite dreamily, "it's Sunday,
right?"

"Yes sir!" a rabbit acknowledged him.

"Hmm," Gum watched over the faces of rabbits
who were lost, confused, and misunderstood. He thought
he needed to put things right and he would.

"Should we get this over with?" Gum said.

17. We do like to get it over with! We really do!

Then, on that Sunday afternoon, as Gum expected, the war was finally called to an end. All plans were all cancelled, and everyone went home to celebrate. Jab and his friends went back to their normal activities and life went on.

After their adventure, a few of Jab's friends did something new to change a part of their lives.

Wallaba started his own arcade game stall where he sneakily went back to the human city and gave a word to a few cats to gather some fun devices to give to him.

Penny also asked the cats to give her some ingredients of some of the human food they had tasted as it had completely changed her.

Apples published his very own book which focussed on his personal journey as he shared his terrifying experience in the human city. There were a few hints that Apples made - a theory of what cats really were, which stunned the readers.

Ricky gave a lecture to a group of rabbits where he shared his views on the human city.

And finally Jab went back to the Rabbit Retrieve and he was about to begin his next mission. But before that, they gave him a worthy rank in their team as he had done something so impossible that he made a name for himself in the Retrieve.

Jab and his friends had a special celebration for the peace, as they remembered the scary, wonderful and outrageous adventure they had.

Over in an open grassy field, a meeting was held with Rag and Gabs. Gum chose this area as he had a deep connection with nature.

Rag heard the news as he was already losing an hour ago. And he hadn't received a word about his brother's whereabouts. He knew Yossi went away and joined the battle; they knew he didn't die on the battlefield, as all the rabbits got better. And they would have recognised him right away.

Gabs was in more shock when he heard the news about Gum. Gabs' connection with the war had drawn him out of line and he was nervous about joining in this meeting.

They were dragged by their associates from their villages to be here as Gum demanded it. Only the three of them with two of their bodyguards were in the fields alone. Two chairs were lined up next to Rag and Gabs. They tried to not make eye contact as it drew awkwardness between them.

"Hmm," Gum spoke as he watched a butterfly going pass his face. "Look at that."

"Leader," Gabs spoke up as his heart pounced. "Why haven't you explained your absence? We split as a nation because of you."

“I do agree,” Rag butted in. “We were going to destroy each other to work out who shall be next in line. And our people were in the middle of it.”

“But there is no need for another Ruler,” Gum told them very suddenly.

“but…”

“There is only one me, and you have to accept that,” Gum told them directly. “I did live up to an age where you may think I’m immortal.”

“But you are!” Gabs said as he knew it was true. “How are we meant to lead if you are gone?”

“Because you will cooperate, even if I am no longer here,” the wise rabbit said. He took a second of silence and enjoyed the nature of their world as it continued to grow. Of the beautiful things it had done and what will come next. “This will be our last meeting.”

"WHAT?!?!" said the two mayors together at once.

"I have new connections to this world. One that all rabbits may not be ready for," the ruler spoke as he wondered deep down, could they really adjust to humankind? They knew some ways now, how to build and evolve, but maybe not yet. "I wish you all the best for the rest of your lives. Even though I won't be part of it."

Then a question came to Rag's mind which he had to know, "so…does that mean neither of us shall claim Ruler?"

"Of course not," Gum told him firmly. "You both failed."

"Failed?!" Gabs asked, shocked. "Failed how?!"

"You didn't come to an agreement with one another. You forced hands to go to war and put the state of our society at risk." Gum thought he would never give the title of Ruler to anyone if it wasn't for those two, but maybe there was someone else. "I would have given this title to your brother, Yossi. He has better experience than you. By the way - where is your brother?"

Across many lands, cities, towns, villages, and islands, across the blizzards of the artic which was frozen with terrible conditions, Yossi made his way to get here. He told his brother that if there was one place he wanted to be in peace, it was here.

But the weather he had to go through wasn't what he had in mind. He imagined it would be an artic escape where he could lay back, lick the red sticky trees, jump in a pool and chill with these opposite animals that weren't rabbit-like. But everything was nothing but cold, dark, miserable, and very blizzardy and he couldn't tell where he was going anymore.

He travelled for weeks and may never return home, which was fine to him, even if he didn't know this. But his brother was really a jerk to him. This was his ending, and this is how endings were made here.

He noticed through the blizzard on the other side, a few feet away from the cold rabbit were two penguins standing in front of their cube home. One was wearing a beany and glasses, and another wore a sweater. The one with the beany sneezed as he had allergies to the snow.

"We thought you looked lost," said the jumper penguin. "We have got hot summer baths that glow orange and red lolly pops which your tongue will never let go." The rabbit stood there as they waited for an answer. "Well, what do you say?"

Yossi had a thought for a moment as he was waiting for something for some time now. Now this was his time for his next chapter.

"Why not?" Yossi said, as he joined the penguins.

The End

Appendix

This Appendix is included for those who are interested in how Liam became an author and how he develops his ideas. Liam hopes that this can create understanding that people with his disabilities can have great things to say and share with the world. Liam also hopes that all those who share his disabilities and want to write can hopefully benefit from learning about how he does it.

Original Outline for Rabbit Rebellion

Below is Liam's original brainstorm/outline for Rabbit Rebellion, created on 9 September 2021, which contains all major plot and character ideas.

THE RABBIT REBELLION

As Humans, We never quite knew about the nature of rabbits and what purpose they bring to our world; why? The Rabbits live in a system of Eco-System and perdure food, plants, and their sitoity to make the rabbit race moving.

With their Ruler Missing, Two Mayors of Two separate Rabbit Villages in the North and the South demand to take control of the Rabbit Race, but with both Mayors fighting off who, they declare to go to War.
Meanwhile, Jab The Rabbit, hears rumors about that they're lost Leader is living in the Human world in the nearby city of London. Jab and a pack of other rabbits embark a adventure of a life time to save they're spices and stop the war.

The Leader, Gum O' Rabbit has been rescued by a Human called Quantise Clan, Gum is a very Old Rabbit but does like the compony of Quantise, but he knew being absent from his Rabbit kind would cause an Anti War.

Jab and his Best Friend Ricky hops over to the City as they try to get a taste of the human world.

The Rabbits inhabit other Human like Tools than they're very own village, they had Carrot Jouesting Swords and they ride on Chickens.

It's Half Meddle-Evil, Half Gangster, Half Summri.

Quantise goes to a Karrti Classes and does go Badly.

Rag is The Major of the Tim Hole Village with his Young Brother Yossi.

Jab's Pals, Wallaba, Apples, Penny and Ricky embark they're adventure.

Jabs and the others go into a street and into a spooky Allyway where they meet Three Skiny Cats hanting them.

Jabs and the others later get caught into a Anmial Rescue Team where they try to escape.

A group of ganster rabbits go into the big city and talk about the Carrot Hill Sight Village Plans and if the others are part of it, they have a rough fight and notice that what the rabbit throw the carrot in his arm isn't dangous at all.

One of the gansters go and hire a sammri to try to assassinate Gabs, the Major of Carrot Hill Sight in the battle zone.

"Oh My! It's some Rouge Wild Chickens hitting our Way!."

Allay way with Cats
Cat Mansion
Shop Center – Arcade
Anmial Conrtol Pen
Pizza Rea
Boat

Epilogue: as Much Yossi wanted to make a fresh start to his rabbit life, he left his idotic brother and goes treavling the glob, and he bumps into some Pangrines in the Artic as he thought he should chill here.
"Yo My Fur" said the Pangrine, "We thought you could come and chill in the Cube House! It has Rad Lolly Pops that your toune would never let go!."
Yossi thought about it and his life before him, "Yeah, why not!."

Example of Liam's unedited writing

A portion of Chapter 9 is reproduced here in Liam's words written as best as he can, before his mum edits.

9) Into the Cat House

Wallaba, Ricky and Penny were taken by eighteen Rouge Cats as they weren't pretty as the other three that Jab, and Apples were with. Ricky and the others were at a street wall near the Old Abandon Mansion that the Cats have been taken over, the Cat House, they call it. These cats take no doubts from the human world; they run and make the rules around these streets. This was their big town, and no one is going to take it, even little rabbits.

The rabbits themselves felt cornered, having so slim chance of escaping. They never imagined a scenario like this would ever happen in the city, they don't have knowledge of what it's really like to be here.

Ricky turns to his friends with a scared look, "I might see you guys at the end of this?", he asks very frightened which his friends said nothing but hummed. They close their eyes as the cats growled and was ready to pouch on them.

Until that is, when a fimler voice which gave them more beyond than hope, "hey guys!." No, it couldn't be they all though as they open their eyes and saw Jab and Apples making their way towards them.

The rouge cats backed away from the three rabbits as they let the more relax two towards them, which the cats seem very concern. Even by Apple's standage, he could tell something was going on.

the grey cat gave the others a look that told them, 'better not feed off them tonight fellas, but maybe another night', which all the cats listen to that demand which seem wasteful to their thoughts.

The thee rabbits were in horror and quite shock about how they're friends could still be alive, "Jab? Apples?", Ricky said stunned.

"its good to see you too, old friend", Jab replied back as he adds a smile, which Ricky and the others share as well, Apples gave a look of terror at all the cats as he thinks he may eat them all, "Hey, they said we could stay here for the night."

"STAY?!", all three rabbits said shockingly beside Apples. They though they'll be dead if they keep lurking around in the area as they thought they were goners not so long ago. Now it's not only seconds they got now to live, but minutes.

"Jab", Ricky spoke both honestly and nervously, "I love your hospitality with other creatures…."

"thank you."

"…But this isn't the wild! You can't trust these guys!."

"Biff! These guys?", Jab said very sure that these felines are nothing than trouble. He knew if they were wolves, they would be dead already, "they invited us, plus they did rescue me and Apples."

"sure, they did", Wallaba commented as he gave an unimpressed look.

"you guys need to know when it comes to gifts from other animals, its hospailty", Jab told them with knowledge, "its rude to not take it. we have to respect their rules and how they run the place. There we can have a better understanding of each other culture."

All the cats were heading inside as Jab gave a positive look at his friends, "this is going to be great, guys!."

The three rabbits stood still for a moment while cats gave glares at them, "shouldn't we tell him about what's really going on?", Penny asked if it would be wise.

"I don't think he knows", Ricky replied, "but I do trust his instincts when it comes to meeting other wildlife. then, I would say we'll follow him, till we see any sort of any trap ahead." The rabbits journey towards the cat house as they went in coarsely

Liam telling his stories through cartoons

(before he could use words well enough to write)

Liam drew pictures from an early age, setting out his stories in his comic form, often divided into chapters. He was prolific in his comic-story drawing all through his childhood. Below is one example of a story.